MURDER AMONG FRIENDS

A Tony Boudreaux Mystery

Other books by Kent Conwell:

The Tony Boudreaux Mystery Series
An Unmarked Grave
The Crystal Skull Murders
Death in the Distillery
Death in the French Quarter
Extracurricular Muder
Galveston
The Puzzle of Piri Reis
Skeletons of Atchafalaya
The Swamps of Bayou Teche
Vicksburg
The Ying in Triad

Angelina Showdown
Atascocita Gold
Bowie's Silver
Grave for a Dead Gunfighter
Gunfight at Frio Canyon
A Hanging in Hidetown
Junction Flats Drifter
Llano River Valley
Promise to a Dead Man
Red River Crossing
The Riddle of Mystery Inn
Shootout on the Sabine
Texas Orphan Train

MURDER
AMONG FRIENDS

•

Kent Conwell

AVALON BOOKS
NEW YORK

Published by Avalon Books,
an imprint of Thomas Bouregy & Co., Inc.
160 Madison Avenue, New York, NY 10016

Library of Congress Cataloging-in-Publication Data

Conwell, Kent.
    Murder among friends / Kent Conwell.
        p. cm.
    ISBN 978-0-8034-7718-6
    1. Boudreaux, Tony (Fictitious character)—Fiction.   2. Private
investigators—Texas—Austin—Fiction.   3. Murder—
Investigation—Fiction.   4. New Mexico—Fiction.   I. Title.
    PS3553.O547M87 2011
    813'.6—dc22
                                                                        2010031087

                PRINTED IN THE UNITED STATES OF AMERICA
                            ON ACID-FREE PAPER
        BY HADDON CRAFTSMEN, BLOOMSBURG, PENNSYLVANIA

*To little Mikey and Keegan, who, while they
keep me young at heart,
keep me mighty sore in muscle*

And to my wife, Gayle

Chapter One

While I've never seen any research on it, I've always believed that most of us, save the very jaded or very selfish, possess one or two of those quixotic genes that drive us to tilt at windmills that we know we can no more defeat than we can lick our elbow.

And that was the very situation I ran into last March when an old friend asked me to do the impossible. Against my better judgment, I gave it a shot and landed neck deep in alligators. Or maybe I should say, neck deep in drifting snow.

You can imagine my surprise that evening when I answered the doorbell at my apartment on Payton-Gin Road and came face to face with an old girlfriend named Debbie Edwards Reeves, a petite brunet with brown eyes that reminded me of Bambi. Like the modern American woman, she was discerning, knowledgeable, and capable; but she was not a multitasker. Give Debbie more than one problem, and she was in trouble.

Don't misunderstand. I have nothing but the highest regard for her even though she is an anachronism, one of those charming and gracious ladies of the South who went out of date fifty years ago. She wears her naïveté well, much too well for a cretin such as myself.

She forced a shy smile. "Hello, Tony."

"Debbie." I glanced over her shoulder, spotting her vehicle parked at the curb. "How—How are you?" It was an awkward remark, but her sudden appearance had surprised me. She was the last person I expected to run in to, although we had dated years ago when we were both teaching at Madison High School in Austin. I'd heard she'd married, and then next thing I heard, they'd split the sheets.

With a terse nod, she dropped her gaze to the ground. "Not so well." She looked up, her brown eyes pleading. "Can I come in? I need some help."

Her words jerked me from my stupor. I pulled the door wide open. I read the papers, and I watched the news, so I knew instinctively why she had knocked on my door. "Sure, sure. Come on in." I indicated the couch. "Have a seat. I'll be right back." While I was wearing a full-length bathrobe cinched in at the waist, I still felt undressed around her. She was the kind that brought out those feelings of decorum most guys have toward their maiden aunts.

Moments later I returned in slacks and polo shirt.

She was sitting on the edge of the couch wringing her hands. From the grimace on her slender face, I knew she had problems, and as much as I hoped against hope, I knew the source of her problems.

A.B., my white cat I'd saved from being used as alligator bait, perched on the back of the couch, eyeing Debbie's short brown hair curiously.

Shooing him away, I plopped down in an easy chair across the coffee table. "Can I get you something: coffee, soft drink?"

Debbie looked up at me, shaking her head. "No. No, thanks." She hesitated, chewing at her bottom lip. "I—I didn't know who else to go to, Tony. I—I've never faced anything like this. This is worse than my divorce."

I listened, hoping I would not hear what I was certain she would say. Perhaps, I told myself, I'm wrong. She's here for another reason. Debbie was one of those sensitive few who become upset by the least incident—a stray cat, a missed dental appointment, a broken fingernail. And truthfully, when we were together years earlier, such concerns were insignificant to me. Still were, in fact. To paraphrase Mark Twain, "concern is an issue of mind over matter. If you don't mind, it doesn't matter." My philosophy indeed.

That had been only one of our problems. After only a short time, I realized I felt nothing for her, at least not what she wanted, not what I wanted. Dating her was like dating my sister, if I had one. I wanted to break up, but she was too decent, too trusting, and too sweet for me to hurt. Fortunately, I left teaching at the end of the year, and we drifted apart.

The few times she'd called, I made excuses about working overtime or being out of town. And yes, I felt like a heel lying to her.

Leaning forward, I laid my hand on hers. "Anything I can do, Debbie. You know that."

She smiled weakly. "It's about my father."

I wanted to close my eyes and groan, but I didn't. Her father had been accused of masterminding an armored car robbery at the credit union of which he was a vice president and disappearing with almost five hundred thousand dollars. I grew somber, hoping against hope she would not ask what I knew she had in mind. "I know. I read about it." I didn't know what else to say. When I read the newspaper purporting him to be the brain behind the half-million-dollar heist, I was stunned. I couldn't believe that was the same Carl Edwards who had helped my mom get her job with the school district over twenty years earlier and then showed her how to join the credit union. Though he was a slightly built man, barely topping five-six, his compassion was that of a giant.

She cleared her throat. "So, you know."

I shrugged, feeling her pain myself. I had my own account at the credit union, and over the years, Carl Edwards and I had become friends, frequently lunching together at a local deli. I'd often wished my old man had been more like Carl. Hey, I'd often wished my old man had just been around. "Yeah. I read the papers." I had a dozen other questions, but I kept quiet.

Her face crumpled and tears welled in her eyes. She fought for control of her voice. "He—He's missing. We don't know where he is. I know it looks bad, but I can't believe Father would do something like that."

In a soft voice, I replied, "The police seem to have a pretty solid case. At least from what I've read in the papers."

Dabbing at her eyes with the corner of a lace handkerchief, she agreed. "But it isn't like Father. He wouldn't do that. He wouldn't steal from anyone, and he wouldn't just vanish without a word. He isn't that kind of man. He's decent, and caring, and honest. You know that."

I smiled sadly at the little girl struggling to defend the man who had always been larger than life to her, who had taken her everywhere with him, who catered to her wishes. If my old man had done any of that with me, I might feel differently about him. "I know. You sure I can't get you something to drink?"

She looked up at me, her eyes red-rimmed. "You can find him for us, Tony. Mother is frantic. The doctor has her on sedatives. I'm afraid she might do something to herself."

While I hurt for her, I could do nothing to help. The armored car heist was an open case, and the police got their noses out of joint when PIs butted in.

"I'll have to talk to my boss, Debbie. I can't do anything on my own." While my remark was the truth, I felt as if I were somehow betraying her.

She looked up at me hopefully and clasped her hands together in front of her. Her face beaming, she gushed, "Thank you, Tony. Thank you. I told Mother we could count on you. You're a wonderful friend."

I felt even guiltier. "Don't get your hopes up. Like I said, I've got to talk to my boss, and he's a stickler for playing by the rules." The last bit stretched the truth, for the fact was Marty Blevins had only one god, other than vodka, and that was money.

After Debbie left, I went online to learn what I could about the heist.

There wasn't much, a couple of articles from the local newspapers. And what I learned was not much more than I had picked up from TV.

The facts alleged that Edwards, accompanied by two men, all wearing gorilla masks, hit the half-million-dollar shipment as the armored car was making its weekly delivery to the Tri-District Credit Union. During the robbery, the second vice president of the credit union, Frank Cooper, was shot by Edwards. Cooper was the one who identified Edwards.

The three vanished. Edwards' car, a new Impala, was never found. Law agencies scoured the city, the county, and the state, but no sign of the three or the vehicle surfaced.

Later, as I lay in bed with A.B. purring away on the next pillow, I couldn't help wondering just what it was that prompted Carl Edwards into such a bizarre scheme. I couldn't argue with Debbie. The Carl Edwards I knew was incapable of such an act. Always smiling, he had an upbeat outlook on life.

Except, I reminded myself, that one time at the end of January when we had lunch together at Lamar Deli. He seemed preoccupied that day even when the waitress served his favorite barbecue, chipped pork. When I asked if something was bothering him, he shrugged. "No. Not really." He shook his head. "A couple problems. One could be—" He shrugged. "Never mind. They'll straighten out." He paused and added, "At least, I hope so." Then he went on to tell me about a fishing trip planned for next month. He gave me a sly grin. "I haven't mentioned it to anyone until I talk to my wife, Margaret, next week. I want to try fly-fishing for bass on Falcon Reservoir on the border. I'm going to talk her into going. Teach her to fly-fish." He studied me for a moment. "You fly-fish? It would be a grand trip."

I'd backed away. I enjoy a relaxing fishing trip, but I can't see anything relaxing about spending a bundle to travel a few hundred miles when I can catch fish within ten miles of where I live.

When I heard of the robbery, I found Edwards' role difficult, no, almost impossible to believe. And even now, when just about everything pointed to him, I still found it hard to accept. Fortunately, I knew Blevins' Security could not get involved in the case.

I sighed with relief, rolled over, and pulled the covers up about my neck, ready for a good night's sleep. Had I known what the next day would bring, I wouldn't have slept at all.

Chapter Two

Before leaving the next morning, I nuked some milk for A.B. and, as usual, left a couple of windows open so the little guy could watch the world go by and let the fresh air tickle his whiskers.

I ducked into my garage and hooked up the battery charger to the 1925 Model T Runabout I'd picked up over in Vicksburg a couple of years back. There was a car show the coming weekend, and Janice Coffman-Morrison, my significant other, who had fallen in love with the Model T, wanted to attend.

Outside, I climbed into my pickup and headed for work at Blevins' Security. I made it a habit of leaving early to beat the traffic, if such is possible in Austin.

The city, a burgeoning metropolis, is well on its way to becoming known as the City with Twenty-Four-Hour Traffic Jams.

I grinned as I thought of Janice.

Her aunt, Beatrice Morrison, CEO of Chalk Hills Distillery, one of Texas' largest producers of fine whiskies, adopted Janice when her parents died in a car crash when she was just a child. Sooner or later, Janice would inherit enough money to pay off half the United States' debt. Well, maybe not half, but a chunk.

We had met a few years earlier when I was working for

an insurance company. I helped her out of a jam, and we became friends.

We dated on occasion, and over the years, sort of began to feel really comfortable around each other. It was a relationship we both preferred until last fall when she brought up the subject of marriage.

About that time, her aunt had a couple of medical problems, and when she healed, she suggested to Janice they take a vacation to the gambling casinos at Monte Carlo. That was the last I'd heard of marriage.

And that was fine with me. I'd been through one divorce and had no inclination for another. And strangely enough, Beatrice Morrison's money did not interest me.

I don't know if fate was playing tricks on me or simply leading me along, but just before I reached the office, Janice called.

As always, she was pleasant and upbeat. Of course, who wouldn't be pleasant and upbeat sitting on one of Texas' largest fortunes? She invited me on a dinner date the next night at the Starlight Room, a newly remodeled Mediterranean restaurant on the top floor of the Commodore Arms, an upscale hotel with a dining and dancing venue overlooking the Colorado River and catering to the very rich in Austin.

"Great," I replied. "What time do you want me to pick you up?"

Her voice bubbling, she replied, "How about nine? That'll give us time to talk."

Time to talk? A cold chill ran up my spine. I managed to croak, "Sounds good. See you then." I punched END, and my life flashed before my eyes.

* * *

Marty had not arrived, which was no surprise. Unless he knew money was waiting, he didn't lumber in until nine-thirty or ten.

I struggled to put Janice out of my mind as I put coffee on the perk and popped down behind my computer to get a head start on the day's mundane task of tailing a joker cheating on his wife.

To my surprise, Marty waddled in fifteen minutes later, informing me he had a nine o'clock appointment that could mean a nice jump in cash flow for the month. His lightweight suit, as usual, was rumpled, as if he'd worn it a week. He hadn't, because the cleaners had delivered it the day before.

"So, what you got today?" He plopped down behind his desk. The chair groaned as he leaned forward and pulled out his ubiquitous bottle of vodka and knocked down a couple of slugs.

I looked on in amazement. A liver as tough as his belonged in the Smithsonian. "Not much. Should nail down the Simmons thing today." He frowned. I explained. "The old boy who's been cheating on his wife."

"Is he?" Marty shrugged.

I nodded and hefted a Canon 440D camera with an EF 70–200 mm lens. "Yep. Got a couple of shots yesterday. A couple more today ought to nail the guy."

He grunted. "Good."

"Yeah. And I've got a decision you have to make. I know the answer, but you're the one who has to give the word."

His pan-shaped face twisted in a frown. "About what?"

I told him about Debbie's visit the night before, mentioning also that she and I had once dated.

He pursed his lips as I went into detail. For some reason, I didn't like the look on his face.

When I finished, he said, "So all they want is for us to find the old boy?"

"Yeah. That's all. But I told her it's an open case with the cops. They aren't going to want us to nose around in it." I paused, and then added, "And I'm not too crazy about it."

"Because you two once dated?"

"Yeah."

Marty studied me a moment, and then shrugged. "You're probably right." He reached for a pen. "Give me her name, and I'll give her a call and explain our position. Don't worry about it."

I should have known that the time to start worrying was when Marty told me not to.

But I didn't. Pushing the next evening with Janice from my mind, I went about my job, tagging after my mark, getting half a dozen shots of the couples' amorous clutches even before they made it into the motel.

A few more shots as they bade each other adieu, and I returned to the office, ran the film through the computer, and dropped it off with our client's lawyer.

When I returned from the attorney's office, Marty called me in and informed me that we could take Debbie Reeves' case.

At first I thought he was joking. "Come on, Marty. It's late, and I'm ready to call it a day."

He poured a shot of vodka and offered it to me. I declined. While I hadn't been attending the AA meetings, I was keeping my vows, most of the time. He slid the bottle back in the drawer. "No joke. I talked to Chief Pachuca at the police station today. Went down to see him, in fact. They have all they need to put Edwards away for a long time. But they can't find him. He'll welcome our help." He paused. "By the way, Reeves and her mother will be in tomorrow at nine to sign the contracts."

I eyed him narrowly. "I don't want the job."

"Huh?" His eyes widened in surprise. "You don't want it? Why not?"

"I told you. Because I know them, and because whatever we find out for them is going to hurt them, and I don't want to be the one doing it."

He shrugged. "Someone's got to do it. If not us, another agency. Besides, being their close friend, you could probably handle it more gracefully than anyone else."

I shook my head and stared at him in wonder. "You don't miss a bet, do you?"

A puzzled frown knit his brows. "What do you mean by that?"

"Nothing," I replied in disgust. "Nothing."

Muttering obscenities under my breath, I headed for my apartment. On the one hand, I couldn't blame Marty. Debbie and her mother were simply another client for Blevins' Security.

Yet, because I had known her so long, and because we had once been fairly close, I wasn't comfortable being the bearer of bad news. I might never find her father, and if I did, he was going to prison. Either way, she wouldn't have him at home. I just didn't want to be the one responsible.

At my apartment, I tossed my tweed jacket on the couch and fell into my evening routine, nuking milk and putting out fresh water and another handful of nuggets for A.B. I was so busy cursing Marty that I failed to notice A.B. wasn't around.

Usually, the little guy was under my feet, weaving back

and forth through my legs like it was his mission on earth to see if he could trip me.

I reached the bathroom before I realized I hadn't seen him, and that's when I spotted the torn screen on the bathroom window.

That window was one of his favorite spots, and I always left it open for him.

I cursed again, and hurried outside. For twenty minutes, I wandered the neighborhood, calling him. Finally, I stood on the corner, my thumbs hooked in the pockets of my washed out jeans, and stared up and down the street.

A neighbor ambled out to the curb. He was an older man who tended his flowerbeds constantly. I guessed him to be in his seventies or so. He waved. "You looking for a white cat?"

I nodded enthusiastically. "Yeah. He got out through a torn screen. You see him?"

"This morning. About ten. Mildred, that's my wife, sent me to the mailbox. I saw a white cat chasing another cat down the street there," he said, pointing east on Payton-Gin Road.

I swore a little more, thanked him, and then climbed in my pickup. I found no sign of A.B.

Back in my apartment, I slammed the door in disgust. First Marty sneaks behind my back and manages to get a case I didn't want; Janice wants to "talk"; and now my cat, the one I saved from being used as alligator bait in a Louisiana swamp, had run off.

"What else could go wrong?" I muttered.

At that moment, the phone rang.

I growled into the receiver. "Yeah?"

"Tony, this is Bob Ray Burrus. We got your old man in jail down here. They say he's involved in some guy's murder."

Chapter Three

Come on, Bob Ray," I replied. "This has been a tough day. I don't need any jokes."

There was no hint of amusement in his voice. "No joke, Tony. John Roney Boudreaux. Brought in this morning passed out. They found him at the rail yards. And they found another guy down there, but he was dead. They figure your father might know something about it. Maybe did it."

I was speechless. After a couple of moments, Bob Ray lowered his voice. "They got no real proof against him, but he was laying there by the dead guy. There was a busted beer bottle near his hand, and the blow to the head is what killed the other dude."

"This other dude, he got a name?"

"The hobos called him Salinas Sal."

In frustration, I muttered, "I can't believe it."

Bob Ray worked the Evidence Room down at the police station. He and I had gone through the first three years at U.T. before he transferred to Sam Houston University at the end of his junior year, changing his major to criminal justice.

He was one of those free-thinking rebels who preferred remaining just within the bounds of convention for the sake of comfort, the comfort of a steady paycheck. From time to time, depending upon how a proposition struck him, he

13

pushed the envelope, even on occasion kicking a hole in it. For the most part, however, he played it straight. Like most uniforms, he wanted his pension.

"I'll be right down."

"Won't do no good, Tony. You know that. He can't go before the judge until morning."

I grimaced. He was right. I should have thought of that, but the telephone call had caught me by surprise, and on top of everything else that was going wrong, the news about my old man was just about one straw away from snapping the back of that proverbial camel. "Thanks, Bob Ray."

I hung up and my eyes shifted to the refrigerator where a chilled bottle of Janice's Merlot lay on the top rack. I chuckled. It had been several months since I'd had the desire for a drink.

Two or three times during the night, I hopped out of bed and hurried to the front door, swearing I heard A.B. clawing to get in. Each time I was disappointed.

The last thing I got that night was a sound sleep. With questions about Debbie's father, my missing cat, Janice's obsession with marriage, and my old man suspected of murder, what little sleep I managed came in snips and snatches.

Before I left home the next morning, I quickly placed all my valuables in the garage with my Model T and locked the door securely against the likelihood that I would be bringing my old man back. The only alcohol in the refrigerator was Janice's Merlot. That was okay. I'd pick up a couple of cases of beer today for my old man.

I popped into the office a few minutes later, informing Marty I would not be at his meeting with Debbie Reeves and her mother. I was in no mood for his clumsy efforts to shame me into attending the meeting for my sake and the company's sake. "No way, Marty," I said, my eyes blazing fire. "I got my old man to worry about. He isn't much, but he is blood kin." I stared into his flat black eyes. "If you don't like it, then fire my tail." I spun on my heel and stormed to the door.

Behind me, Marty stuttered and stammered. "Hey. Tony! I didn't mean it like that. Go right ahead. I'll fill you in when you get back." Good old Marty. He was as flexible and adaptable as duct tape.

Half a dozen denizens of the street slouched on the bench in front of Judge Simon. I knew the judge, and he was a fair man—a hard one, but fair.

I studied the backs of the defendants, unable to pick out my old man. After all, I told myself, it had been several months, almost a year, since I last saw him. I paused and chuckled wryly to myself. The last time I saw him was when he robbed me blind and pawned the goods for booze.

Bob Ray Burrus stood at my side. He pointed to the second set of slumped shoulders. "That's him."

"Thanks," I muttered, moving to the side for a better look at his angular face.

We got lucky. I don't know if it was because the Austin PD didn't want to have to put up with John Roney for several months until a trial, or because the judge knew me and realized I would have my old man to trial when and if it came up, or because the evidence against him was pretty flimsy, but I got my old man out on a two-thousand-dollar bond.

I never liked riding with my old man. He never bathed, and even with the windows down, the stench was enough to gag a dog on a gut wagon. And that thirty minutes back to my place was no different.

But during that drive, I told my old man in no uncertain terms that if he left my apartment, I would be the first to turn in his sorry tail to the police. And if I did, he might as well never expect any help from me again.

The frail man looked around at me. "That ain't a kindly thing to do to your old man, boy."

I snorted. "Come on, John. Every time I've helped you, it's ended up with you pawning half my stuff so you can buy your cheap Thunderbird wine."

He frowned, feigning hurt feelings. "That ain't so. A couple times, I used the money for train fare."

All I could do was shake my head and roll my eyes.

I picked up a six-pack of Old Milwaukee beer from a convenience store before we reached my apartment. Leaving the pickup door open to air out, I escorted my old man inside, pointing out the shower and my dresser of clean garments, and suggesting he take advantage of them. "Toss your clothes in the washer. I'll run them though the cycle tonight. TV dinners are in the freezer."

He nodded, but from the glaze over his eyes, I knew the first thing he would do was open a beer, guzzle a couple of swallows, and then pass out on the couch.

I wagged a finger at him. "Remember. Don't go anywhere. I'll find out what I can about what they have against you. Then we'll have a better idea of where we stand. I left my cell number and office number on the pad by the phone. Call me if you need anything."

It was noon before I reached the office. To my surprise, Debbie and her mother were waiting patiently for me.

Debbie's eyes lit when she saw me. Both ladies rose quickly. Debbie hurried to me and threw her arms around me. "Thank you, Tony. Thank you. I knew I could depend on you." Before I could reply, she gestured to the older woman at her side. "You remember Mother."

There was no question from whom Debbie had inherited her physical attributes. Margaret Edwards was perhaps a few pounds heavier, but still a striking woman. The black business outfit she wore was as conservative as it was becoming. She smiled and extended her hand. "Hello, Tony. Nice to see you again."

I glanced around for Marty, but he was nowhere to be seen. One of his typical moves, vanish until tempers cool. "Thank you, Mrs. Edwards." I hesitated, looking from one to the other.

Debbie must have seen the puzzlement on my face, for she explained, "We gave Mr. Blevins all the information this morning, but when he said you had volunteered to handle the case, we decided to go over it again, this time with you in case there are any questions we didn't make clear."

"I see." I drew a deep breath. "That's a good idea." I glanced around the empty office. "I haven't had lunch yet. Would you ladies care to join me?"

Longhorn Mall, across the street from our office, housed several eatcries. We opted for Luby's Cafeteria, carrying our trays out onto the colonnade where we found a table away from the crowd.

I love good food, but I learned years ago that too much red beans and rice, too much jambalaya, or too much berry cobbler were bad for the waistline. I had a salad.

Debbie and her mother must have believed as I did, for they each had a small Jell-O and tea.

"So," I said before taking a bite of my salad. "Tell me all that happened at the credit union."

They looked at each other. Mrs. Edwards nodded. "Go ahead, Debbie."

In a soft voice, she began. "On February 3, the armored car that was making its regular delivery to the Tri-District Credit Union was robbed. It carried half a million dollars. There were three men. They all wore masks. Frank Cooper, the second vice president, was shot. He said father was the one who shot him."

I frowned. Around a mouthful of salad, I asked, "If they wore masks, how did he identify your father?"

"By his voice." She paused.

"And his coat. It was herringbone. The suit was herringbone," added Mrs. Edwards.

Debbie continued. Most of her story I had read online. Her father had vanished, along with his 2009 Impala. What made it so peculiar was that he had no apparent financial problems. His investments were sound, although, as with all investments, subject to the capriciousness of the stock market. He and his wife were planning a vacation to London, England, the next Christmas, a dream the two had shared for decades.

Oh, yes, he had also mentioned to me that he was planning a spring fishing trip to Falcon Reservoir.

According to Debbie, The police had hit a wall in tracking him down. The only hint of his destination was a plane ticket to San Francisco.

I frowned. "Why San Francisco?"

Debbie shrugged. "I—We don't know."

"You mean he didn't tell you where he was going and why?"

With a hint of color in her cheeks, she smiled shyly. "Father never told us about business. He didn't want us to worry."

When she told me that, I whistled softly.

Debbie and her mother frowned. I explained, "San Francisco is where everyone goes to disappear."

Mrs. Edwards' brows knit. "You don't think you can find him?"

I studied the two of them, seeing the pain in their eyes. I hated hurting people, but at the same time, I didn't want to give them too much hope. "To be honest, Mrs. Edwards, it won't be easy. But we'll give it a shot. What I can promise is that we'll run down every lead until there's nothing left to run down." I paused, remembering his spring fishing trip. "Did your husband ever mention anything about Falcon Reservoir on the U.S.–Mexico border?"

She frowned and pondered the question. Slowly, she shook her head. "Not a word. Why?"

"I don't know. The week before the robbery, we had lunch at a deli, and he told me was going to see if you wanted to go there with him. He seemed to think that would be a nice place to retire."

Mrs. Edwards winced, and then shook her head. "He never mentioned it to me."

"No problem," I replied. "It was just a guess." I smiled at her. "Don't worry. I'll check it out."

She nodded, and then glanced nervously at Debbie. She cleared her throat. "We've thought about calling in a psychic. Have you ever had any dealings with one, Tony?"

A psychic? I wanted to tell her to save her money. I've never bought into the idea. If someone can see into the future, why are they advertising in the Yellow Pages or living in the shabby part of town? Psychics reminded me of the tarot card readers and mediums on the esplanades around Jackson Square in New Orleans' French Quarter, all hustlers. The only way they can bend a spoon is with both hands.

All I could do was shake my head. "Sorry. I've never had any experience with them."

Chapter Four

It was two o'clock by the time we finished lunch. I still found it difficult to believe Carl Edwards masterminded the job. That's why when I pushed back from the table, I asked one last question, a shot in the dark, but one that might point me in a direction besides Edwards. "Did Mr. Edwards ever mention anyone at the credit union who was in financial straits?"

The two women frowned at each other, and then Mrs. Edwards shook her head. "Never. Carl was not the kind to bring the job home."

After seeing them to their vehicle, I climbed in my pickup and pulled out the ubiquitous three-by-five cards on which I took notes. I quickly jotted down what I had learned from Debbie and her mother. While doing so, I realized I didn't believe Edwards was guilty. Despite what had been written and said, he was not the kind of man to do what he was accused of.

I'm no PI whiz, not like my co-worker, Al Grogan. Al is one of those with an instinctive knack for deduction. I personally think he would be a fair match even for Sir Arthur Conan Doyle's fictional Sherlock Holmes. Over the years, I've picked up some of Al's habits, although mine are not honed to the same keen edge as his. One caveat he preached that I observed religiously was to explore in detail everyone concerned with the crime. Suspect everyone. Give everyone the most sinister of motives. Then as you investigate, you can modify, but start off as if all were guilty, a difficult task for a little Catholic boy brought up to trust everyone.

I paused in jotting down my notes and stared, unseeing, through the windshield. I would start with the credit union, but I could not interview them as if they were suspect. If I did that, Chief Ramon Pachuca of the Austin P.D. would have my head.

I planned on questioning each employee as to whether he had any idea where Edwards might have gone. Maybe something would turn up there. Of course, I knew that people being people, some of them would be offended or insulted, and perhaps become belligerent.

That meant I had to have the backing of Chief Pachuca. You know, use his name like a shotgun if I had to.

Starting the pickup, I headed downtown, planning on taking out two birds with one shot: find out where the investigation against my old man stood and pay the chief a visit.

I'd been in the business several years, long enough to establish a few contacts. One of the investigators for the district attorney was Mark Swain, who had attended U.T. with me and Bob Ray Burrus. After school, he'd joined the police force and worked on his law degree at U.T. On several occasions, our paths had crossed and, on a couple of them, I turned out to be of help to him.

I caught Mark in the hall outside the office, hurrying to an elevator. He motioned me to follow. "I've got court in five minutes. What's up?"

As the elevator doors slid shut, I told him about my old man. He frowned. "Haven't heard a thing. Of course, that's not unusual. It takes a few days for us to get the paperwork." The elevator jerked to a halt. The doors hissed open. "I say don't sweat it for a week or so. Just make sure your old man hangs around. A murder, you say?"

"He was found next to a dead transient. Near his hand was a broken beer bottle they say was the murder weapon."

Mark paused at the courtroom door and straightened his jacket. "If I hear something, I'll give you a call."

Chief Pachuca was just as accommodating. He and I had been on a couple of cases together, but I had always made it a point never to interfere with police business. More than once, I went to him with evidence I had turned up. Sometimes it served him well. And he never forgot it.

"Yeah. Go ahead. Tell what's-his-name over there at the credit union, the president, Lindsey, to give me a call if he wants. We got all we need on Edwards to convict him. All that's missing is the man."

"No idea where he might have gone?"

"Nope. A week earlier, he bought a ticket on a seven o'clock American flight on February 3 to San Francisco, but he didn't make it." He chuckled. "You want to know how dumb the guy is? He used his own name."

"Oh?" I wanted to ask more, but I knew better.

Pachuca continued, "My people studied the film from the boarding camera a dozen times. He never checked in. He might have figured we'd be watching the flights and backed out." He paused and glared up at me. "Satisfied?"

I cleared my throat. With a crooked grin, I asked, "I don't suppose I could see what you have, could I?"

He looked at me in disbelief, but when he saw the grin on my face, he shook his head and waved me away. "Get out of here before I change my mind."

* * *

"No! No, no, no." Raiford Lindsey, president of Tri-District Credit Union, was livid. His pan-shaped face grew red, and if I could have seen the veins in his fleshy neck, there's no doubt they would have been distended like a balloon ready to pop. He sputtered, "We've had enough trouble over the robbery. I don't want to drag it up all over again. Besides, we know who did it. I don't want it to look like any of the other employees are suspected of being involved."

In a soft, calm voice, I explained. "I'll make it a point to reassure them, Mr. Lindsey. All I'm saying is that sometime in the past, Carl Edwards might have inadvertently suggested a destination to one of them. You know, an ideal vacation spot, a hidden retreat." That wasn't the whole truth, but I figured it would be enough to keep the guy from dropping dead in his office from a heart attack.

His eyes blazing, he studied me a moment.

I lied some more. "I don't believe any of your employees were involved. Okay? I'm just looking for leads as to Edwards' whereabouts. As I said, Chief Pachuca okayed this. Call him if you want."

He studied me several more moments, and then drew in a deep breath and released it. He cleared his throat. "I don't like it, but all right. I just don't want my people upset." He paused, and then added, "I still can't believe it. Carl—well, I was stunned." He paused and shook his head. "Just goes to show you. You never can tell."

If I've heard that old platitude once, I'd heard it a thousand times. Nodding sympathetically, I replied, "I understand. Now, if I can have a roster of your employees."

He grimaced. "Sure. Sure." He punched the speaker on the telephone. "Ms. Romero, bring me a roster of all employees." He hesitated, glanced at me, and added, "Addresses, phone numbers, all we have."

There were forty-two names on the list. I whistled softly.

When I pulled out of the credit union parking lot, I glanced at my watch. Almost five. Time to get back to my old man. But first I wanted to drop off a copy of the list to Danny O'Banion, my link, however tenuous, with the mob. Interviewing forty-two individuals would take a couple of weeks. I needed to narrow down the list if I could. Besides, I reminded myself, in just a few hours, I had to pick up Janice.

My mind raced. I was concerned about my father, but for the time being, he was not my primary worry. Mark Swain had said to sweat nothing for a week. What really puzzled me was Janice. She wanted to talk, and in my experience with the fairer gender, whenever they wanted to *talk*, the outcome was usually unpleasant.

I drew a deep breath. I could sure use a drink about now. I glanced at the back of my seat. In the past, I'd kept a bottle behind the pickup seat, accessible only if I stopped. But a few weeks earlier in a burst of righteous passion after an AA meeting, I'd dumped it. I'd dumped them all except Janice's bottle of wine. Now I was calling myself every name in the book for being such an idiot.

I headed downtown to Danny O'Banion's office on the top floor of the Green Light Parking Garage. Rumor was that Danny was Austin's *caporegime*.

I knew the truth, but I never said a word about it. Danny and I go back to high school, where in the eleventh grade, we managed to get into a few scrapes together.

He dropped out of school, and I ended up an English

teacher, then an insurance salesman, and finally a private investigator.

Later, Danny and I ran into each other at an Oklahoma–U.T. football game in Dallas. We laughed some, lied a lot, and emptied his silver flask of excellent Scotch.

From time to time over the years, Danny gave me a few hints on cases I had. I paid him back when I managed to save his cousin, Bobby Packard, from the needle up in Huntsville.

Today was one of those days I needed his help.

After making a copy of the list Raiford Lindsey had supplied me, I pulled into the multistory parking lot where Danny had his office.

He greeted me with a large grin and a big hug.

He poured a straight bourbon, and I poured a straight water. He studied the list. "So you want to know if any these bozos got any reason to hit the armored car, huh?"

"That's it," I nodded.

Giving me that little leprechaun grin of his, he replied, "Why don't you just talk to all of them?"

I rolled my eyes and gestured to the length of the list. "Not if I can help it. I don't have two or three weeks to spare."

He chuckled. "No sweat. I'll send it out to your place when I finish."

"Thanks." Then I remembered my old man. "On second thought, give me a call. I'll pick it up." A frown knit his freckled forehead. I explained the situation. "He'd probably flush it down the toilet."

To my relief, my old man was still home. He'd downed the whole six-pack of Old Milwaukee, but he was still home. To my dismay, he wore the same clothes, and I had to throw open the windows to air out the place.

Luckily, I had the foresight to pick up a couple of pepperoni and cheese pizzas and a case of beer on the way in.

John Roney ignored the piping hot pizza, preferring the beer. I nodded to his ragged garments. "No beer until you get out of those so I can wash them. I'll get you some stuff to wear, and then you can have the beer."

In less than two minutes, he'd done as I suggested and, in a set of baggy sweats, was nursing a cold beer. I tossed his clothes in the washer.

Setting him on the couch, I grilled him on the incidents at the railway station.

He looked at me blankly. His ragged whiskers clung to his sunken cheeks. He slurred his words. "I don't remember nothing. A bunch of us come in from San Antone. Kansas City Mort had managed a couple bottles of wine. We done drunk it down, and I don't remember nothing 'til I woke up in the drunk tank."

He reached for his beer, but I grabbed his bony wrist. "Listen to me. I'm doing my best to keep you from spending the rest of your—" I started to say worthless because that's all he'd ever been to me, but somehow, the word refused to roll off my lips. "The rest of your life in prison," I said.

He looked up at me, and I would have sworn he had no idea what I was talking about. I continued, "Did you know someone on the trains by the name of Salinas Sal?"

He cocked his head. "Sal? Yeah. I know Sal. We rode from Oregon down to Arizona and then over to San Antone together. What about him?" His eyes drifted back to the beer on the coffee table.

I jerked on his wrist, forcing him to look at me. "Someone killed him here in Austin, and the cops think you're the one who did it."

He stared at me and muttered. "Not me."

"What do you know about it?"

"Nothing." He shook his head. "Last I seen Sal, he was heading for Sixth Street. That's when Kansas City Mort come up with the wine. We sat under the loading docks and drunk it down."

Chapter Five

Passing through downtown on the way to Janice's ranch, I spotted one of the winos who lived in the alleys and deserted buildings along Sixth Street. Whenever transients jumped off the train in the Austin rail yard, they usually found their way downtown.

Possibly, I told myself, as I wended through the traffic flowing south, I might run across one or two who knew about the killing. I'd check with them later.

Normally, the winding drive along Bee Tree Road that cut through the oak- and cedar-covered hills west of Austin was pleasant and relaxing. Tonight, my mind was tiptoeing gingerly around the subject of marriage. I had rehearsed a small speech, one I felt was firm enough to deter marriage, yet understanding enough not to hurt Janice's feelings.

At the top of the last hill, I looked down at Chalk Hills Distillery, a collection of white stucco buildings with bright red roofs of Spanish tile.

The main house sat at one end of the compound, surrounded by a magnificent landscape that over the years had graced the covers of half a dozen national magazines.

Looking back, I know now I was a little too full of myself,

for I muttered, "There it is, Tony. All yours for the asking." But I wasn't about to ask.

I waited in the library, visiting with her aunt, Beatrice Morrison. I remembered the first time I met her. Her thin frame was ramrod straight and her demeanor regal. I had thought at the time she would have made a striking Cleopatra, a tad old perhaps, but striking anyway. And the last few years, if anything, had enhanced the intimidating sovereignty of her majesty.

As always, our conversation was awkward and stiff. "How are you, Aunt Beatrice?" Though she had requested I address her as such, I always had the feeling she cringed inside when a commoner such as myself called her "aunt."

She sniffed and deigned me with a glance. "Well, Tony. You?"

"Fine, just fine, Aunt Beatrice."

"Good. Glad to hear that."

"Nice weather."

"Yes, it is."

"Might rain."

"It might."

And such a scintillating exchange of witty repartees continued until Janice showed up, which she did almost immediately, bringing a merciful end to our conversation.

Janice, as usual, was a knockout. All I knew about the labels on her dress or shoulder wrap was they did not come from K-Mart or Penney's.

She crossed the room to her aunt. "Good night, Aunt Beatrice." She touched her lips to her aunt's cheek. "I'll be in early."

She turned to me, and with a bright smile handed me the

keys to her Jag. "You drive, Tony. I don't want to ride in that pickup of yours with my good clothes." She slid her arm through mine. I had no idea what perfume she wore, but it was tantalizing and tempting.

And I didn't mind going in her car. I loved driving the Jaguar roadster. During the drive to the Starlight Room in downtown Austin, we made idle chitchat. Each time the conversation lulled, my heart dropped to the pit of my stomach, thinking the next words that rolled from her lovely lips would be marriage.

But, to my surprise, she mentioned nothing about it.

I did not recognize the remodeled Starlight Room at the Commodore Arms. The only things that were familiar were the prices.

We enjoyed a few cocktails, appetizers of flavored olives and baba ghanoush, and several dances before ordering. When our server came to take our order, Janice clapped her hands like a little girl and said, "Let me order for us, Tony. Aunt Beatrice and I had some wonderful dinners on our Mediterranean cruise."

I sipped my cocktail and smiled at her. "Go right ahead."

She nodded to our server and ordered chicken Provençal with artichokes and garlic, toasted Israeli couscous pilaf with onions, and zucchini boats filled with caramelized onions, pesto, and Romano cheese.

Throughout dinner, she bubbled with conversation, not once mentioning the word *marriage*. I was beginning to wonder if I had gotten a little too bigheaded for my own good.

By midnight, when we climbed in her Jag and headed back to the ranch, I had pushed my concerns aside. Once we hit Bee Tree Road, she scooted around in the seat and laid her hand on my shoulder. "Remember when I said I wanted us to talk, Tony?"

For a fleeting second, I froze. If someone had offered me a million dollars to turn the wheel of the little Jag half an inch one way or another, I couldn't have done it. Finally, I found my voice. "Yeah. Yeah, I remember." But what I couldn't remember was the little speech I'd rehearsed and rehearsed for this very situation, telling her she was too good for me.

I kept my eyes fixed on the dark and winding road ahead of us. She continued. "You know a few months ago, when you were down in San Antonio, we talked about marriage."

"Yeah, I remember." But I didn't. In fact, my entire past had gone blank. I was starting to sweat.

We started down the hill toward the main house. Her tone grew serious. "Then Aunt Beatrice went to the hospital."

That I remembered. "Yeah."

"Luckily, it was nothing serious, but it made me stop and realize that she needs me. I'm her only family. I couldn't leave her by herself." She squeezed my arm. Her voice tense, she asked, "You understand what I'm saying, Tony?"

I had to blink my eyes once or twice. I wasn't sure if I did or not, but I lied. "Yeah. I understand. Sure, I do."

The tense stress fled her voice. Her words bubbled. "Wonderful. I just didn't want to hurt your feelings. I think the world of you, but marriage isn't something I think I should enter into right now."

I pulled into the circular drive and stopped the Jag in front of the main entrance and turned off the ignition. For several seconds, I sat staring out the front window.

Her voice was a whisper. "Tony, Tony. Are you all right?" She laid her slender fingers on my arm. "You're sweating."

I should have been elated, but for some inexplicable

reason, I was confused. I forced a wide grin. "Sure. I'm fine, and I understand. Don't you worry about it."

She smiled brightly and hopped out of the small roadster. "Fine. And don't forget about Sunday."

With a terse nod, I replied, "Charging the battery on the car now."

Her eyes glittered in the porch lights. "Just leave the Jag here. One of the boys will put it up."

After escorting her to the huge double doors and giving her a light goodnight kiss, I stumbled woodenly back to my pickup. Slowly, the realization dawned on me that Janice had dumped me. That wasn't how it was supposed to work. I was supposed to reject her, not be the dumpee.

The drive back to my apartment on the north side of Austin was the longest drive in my life. The left side of my brain was bouncing around and shouting in glee, while the right side wallowed in the quicksand of misery.

Chapter Six

A dark Lincoln Town Car was parked in front of my apartment when I pulled into the drive. I recognized it as Danny's. The door opened, and a behemoth in a Nicky Hilton suit lumbered out. The big vehicle seemed to spring up six inches when he exited.

Huey. Danny's bodyguard. A body double for Godzilla.

As always when I met him, I grinned and held up my hand. "Hey, Huey."

The first time I had seen Huey was one night on a narrow road west of Austin. At the time, his square face looked like a chunk of chipped granite, square, solid, with no distinguishing features other than a couple of fissures for eyes, a square knob for a nose, and a third crevice that was probably his mouth. His face hadn't changed over the years, still full of knobs and fissures.

A grunt escaped his thin lips, and he held out an envelope. "Danny says I should give you this."

"That was fast."

The compliment didn't faze him. Without a word, he turned back to the Lincoln. I could have sworn I felt the ground shake. "Tell Danny I said thanks."

His only reply was a faint nod.

The Lincoln sagged when he slipped behind the wheel.

* * *

Sprawled on the couch, my old man's ragged snoring was a nerve-wracking counterpoint to the blaring TV. I flipped it off, wishing I could do the same with his snoring, but I reminded myself, if I disturbed him, he might wake up, and I much preferred him when he slept.

I wrinkled my nose. He still hadn't bathed or shaved.

Shaking my head, I went into the bathroom for a bottle of after-shave lotion, which I sprinkled liberally about the living room. From there, I headed for the kitchen where I retrieved a can of sweet tea from the refrigerator and plopped down at the snack bar to peruse the information Danny had provided.

Of the forty-two names, he had placed a check mark beside five and, in his inimitable scribbling, made a few notes on the back of each page. He cautioned me that these five were the only ones with whom he or his boys had knowledge.

Now, I'm not naïve enough to believe there's no gambling in Austin or in any other city in the state just because it's illegal. The fact it is against the law makes it that much more exciting. Still, I marveled to myself as I studied the list, I had no idea illegal gambling was so extensive.

The first name on the list was Mary Louise Smith, one of the loan officers and a regular at the local but illegal dog and pony OTB rooms. Two weeks earlier, she had paid off a fifteen-thousand-dollar marker.

Another loan officer, Rita Johnson, was a two- or three-time-a-month visitor to the gambling boats in Lake Charles, Louisiana. Sometimes her husband accompanied her.

Then there was Marvin Busby, in charge of business loans, who currently owed one of the local card games eight thousand dollars.

The vice president of Finance, Larry Marion Athens, was a dedicated gambling boat player, sometimes making as many as half a dozen trips a month to casinos outside of the state.

And to my surprise, the last one was Raiford Lindsey's executive secretary, Elizabeth Romero, a ten-year member of the private club Omar's. I'd heard of Omar's. It was one of those widespread secrets that nobody admits knowing. Just about any game a person preferred, he could find there.

I gulped down the remainder of the tea and shook my head and studied the list. Not much, but at least it was a starting place. I yawned and stretched my arms over my head. I was ready for bed.

On impulse, I stuck my head out the door and called A.B. No answer. I called again. Still no answer. "Maybe in the morning," I muttered, knowing deep inside that next morning there would be only an empty doorstep.

After showering, I plopped down in front of my computer and scanned the list of employees into a file.

Over the years, I had acquired several computer skills enabling me to run down missing persons with a fair degree of success, but none of my meager efforts could begin to match those of Eddie Dyson.

Once Austin's resident stool pigeon, Eddie Dyson had become a computer whiz and wildly successful entrepreneur.

Instead of sleazy bars and greasy money, he found his niche for snitching in the bright glow of computers and comforting security of credit cards. Any information I couldn't find, he could. Personally, I figured he hacked into some kind of national database. What kind, I have no idea, but he always came up with information, information that suggested his total disregard of the principles of the 1988 Privacy Act.

There were only two catches if you dealt with Eddie. First, you never asked him how he did it, and second, he only accepted VISA credit cards for payment.

I never asked Eddie why just VISA. Seems like any credit card would be sufficient, but considering the value of his service, I never posed the question. As far as I was concerned, if he wanted to be paid in Polish zlotys or Guatemalan quetzals, I'd load up a couple dozen bushels and send them to him.

Failure was not a word in his vocabulary. His services did not come cheap, but he produced. Sometimes the end is indeed worth the means.

In my e-mail, I requested background checks on the five Danny picked out as well as the credit union president, Raiford Lindsey and the second vice president, Frank Cooper. Hesitating, I glanced at the remainder of the list. I wanted more, but I wasn't certain just on what criteria to focus Eddie's search.

With a shrug, I clicked SEND. I could pull up public records on the others. No telling what I might find.

I glanced at my old man. He was still sleeping. I made a mental checklist of things to do the next day as I crawled between the sheets.

I decided to start with Frank Cooper, the second vice president and the one Edwards shot.

Next morning, Raiford Lindsey's round face grew red when I told him I wanted to conduct my interviews on the premises. I explained that it would be much simpler as well as much more expedient for me to visit with them at work than string it out over a couple of weeks. "You want it over with, and I want it over with. The sooner it's done, the sooner I'm gone."

He studied me a moment, and then nodded. "All right. You can use the conference room at the end of the hall. Tell my secretary, Ms. Romero, who you want to see." He picked up the receiver and buzzed her. "I'll tell her you're coming."

At the mention of her name, I decided to interview her first.

Tastefully dressed in a mauve business suit with white blouse and lacy collar about her throat, Elizabeth Romero appeared to be in her fifties, perhaps fifty-five I guessed as I looked down at her. A few strands of gray accented her dark hair that lay on her shoulders. She didn't look like a seasoned gambler. Though she was seated, I guessed she was a few inches over five feet and about a hundred and ten pounds. For some reason, I noted she was smaller than Carl Edwards.

She nodded to the telephone on her desk and smiled up at me. "How can I help, Mr. Boudreaux?"

I smiled warmly. "I'd like to visit with you a few minutes, Ms. Romero. Mr. Lindsey said it would be all right."

The smile on her face froze. She shot a puzzled glance at the closed door to his office. "I know he said to call some of our employees in, but—"

Giving her my best little-boy grin, I finished her sentence for her. "But you didn't know I meant you also, right?"

She nodded, her eyes shifting uncomfortably.

"Look," I said. "We can talk right here. It's just that you're in this position to know probably more about the credit union than anyone, Mr. Lindsey included."

She couldn't resist a faint smile at the obvious flattery. "Well, yes, but—"

I took a chair beside her desk. "It won't take long."

Running the tip of her tongue over her lips, she drew a deep breath. Her face remained taut. "Well, all right."

"Good. Now, all I'm trying to do is find out if anyone has an idea where Carl Edwards might have gone. Did you know him well?"

A sense of relief washed over her. "Oh, yes. Carl was a gentleman, something you don't find much of today. When I heard what had happened, I couldn't believe it. That was the last thing I would have expected."

"How long have you known him?"

"Over twenty-five years. He was here when I came."

"So, over that time, you got to know him pretty well, huh?"

The tenseness in her face continued to fade. "Yes. And that's what puzzles me. Carl seemed content with what he had. I never once heard him dreaming about a better life. If he told me once, he told me a hundred times that the good Lord had blessed him with everything he could desire. Why, that last day, he was telling me about the birthday present he was getting for his wife. He could barely talk with laryngitis because he was wheezing and hacking from a bad cold, but he had to tell me about the diamond broach he was getting her." Tears welled in her eyes. She dabbed at them with a Kleenex and muttered. "I'm sorry."

"Don't be. Just a couple more questions. Is there anyone around that he was fairly close with, that he might have shared a few secrets with?"

Chewing on her bottom lip, Elizabeth furrowed her brow. "Not really. Well, maybe Marla Jo Keeton." She hesitated and glanced around, and then leaned forward. "She's divorced. Been here almost thirty years. She's in accounting. Like all of us—" She paused and gave me a sheepish grin. "This is just between you and me, isn't it? I mean, confidential?"

I smiled. "Naturally."

She drew a deep breath. "Well, like all of us more mature people, she had problems transitioning to the computer, but she did an excellent job. Took her a little longer, but she hung in there. A couple of years later came her divorce, and she went off the deep end. Alcohol. About ten years ago, Carl helped her get into a rehab. It was either that or lose her job here. She completed rehab successfully." A faint smile played over her lips. "And thank the Lord, she's never fallen back. Carl always made it a point to visit with her."

"One other question. The armored car delivery. Was that a special or routine delivery?"

"Just routine."

"So, I could say that everyone knows when it's due, right?"

She frowned at me, and then nodded. "Yes." She paused, frowned, and then added. "We always video the transfer of funds, but that day, someone cut off the video." I lifted an eyebrow in question. She shrugged. "It must've been Mr. Edwards."

I wanted to pursue the video, but decided to wait. I rose. "Thanks."

Arching an eyebrow, she said. "That's it?"

"That's it. Painless, huh?" I hooked my thumb down the hall in the direction of the conference room. "Now, if you can send Frank Cooper to see me, I'd appreciate it."

She arched an eyebrow. "Frank's out. He'll be back later this morning."

"Fine. Send him then. In the meantime, what about Ms. Keeton?"

Her smile grew wider. "Right away."

Chapter Seven

Marla Jo Keeton was a short, plump woman who might have topped five feet on tiptoes. I guessed she was a tad older than Elizabeth Romero. Her hair was pulled back in a severe bun on the back of her head. She stared at me, her eyes narrowed in suspicion.

I introduced myself and offered her a chair. Quickly, I explained the purpose of my visit. The suspicion faded from her eyes. "I'll be honest, Mr. Boudreaux. That man saved my life. Even if I knew where he was, which I don't, I wouldn't tell you." She paused.

Chuckling with admiration at her candor, I remarked, "He must have been a good friend."

"The best." Her brow wrinkled. "I can't believe he would do such a thing. When I heard about it, I figured it was a mistake."

So far, everyone with whom I'd spoken voiced the same sentiments, my own sentiments. On impulse I said, "Tell me something, Ms. Keeton. If this was an inside job, and Carl Edwards had no part in it, is there anyone else who might have?"

She looked at me in surprise.

Before she could reply, I continued. "I know there are some employees who like to gamble. I know there are some in debt." I paused and waited for her reaction.

41

The roly-poly little woman eyed me skeptically. "I thought you were interested only in finding him, not solving the robbery?"

Her perceptive response surprised me. With a shrug, I said, "The robbery is solved, Ms. Keeton. The police say it was Carl Edwards." I paused. "Maybe I shouldn't have asked the question. If I offended you, I apologize."

She nodded slowly. "Don't worry about it. All I can say is that there are some around here that wouldn't surprise me if they had a hand in something like that."

Keeping an uninterested expression, I replied, "Oh? Such as?"

She hesitated. "Understand, I'm not saying he had anything to do with it, but I heard that Marvin Busby is in a financial squeeze."

I played dumb. "Busby. Now let's see, he's in—" I stammered deliberately.

"Business loans," she blurted out. She glanced nervously at the closed door, and then added. "He's been going out with one of our tellers, Judith Perry. She might be able to tell you more."

I thanked her. As she left, my cell rang. The call was from Debbie Edwards Reeves. She and her mother were meeting a psychic at their home at three o'clock that afternoon. They wanted me there.

Before leaving the credit union, I called Elizabeth Romero and arranged to visit with Smith and Johnson the next morning. Then that afternoon, I'd interview Athens and Busby. I had other plans for Judith Perry.

I glanced back over my list of names.

At that moment, the door opened, and a bronzed man

straight out of *Gentleman's Quarterly* extended his hand. "Tony Boudreaux? I'm Frank Cooper. Raiford said you were here. I wanted to meet you."

Everything about Cooper was neat, from his carefully parted hair to his brightly shined shoes. There was no doubt in my mind that the crease in his slacks would slash a careless finger.

I glanced down at my tweed jacket, Polo shirt, and washed out jeans. I took his hand and nodded. "Mr. Cooper."

His amiable smile beamed. "Call me Frank."

"All right, Frank."

"I wanted to visit with you before you left, but looks like you're getting ready to cut out."

"Yeah. Got another appointment."

He slapped me on the shoulder. "Why, hey. I'll walk you out to your car."

"Fine with me." As we started down the hall, I said, "You're the one Edwards shot, right?"

He grimaced. "Yeah. Sure surprised me." He chuckled. "In more ways than one. Never would have expected that from Carl."

"What happened?"

"It was February 3, a Wednesday. The armored car arrived just after two, a few minutes late. The head teller usually handles the delivery, but Carl decided to do it that day." He shrugged. "I didn't think anything about it. From time to time, one of us will do it. In fact, things were kind of slow that day, so I thought I'd look on. Kill some time, you know?" He grinned. "No pun intended."

As he continued, I glanced at the teller windows, spotting Judith Perry, a willowy brunet around five-two or so with laughing eyes and an animated smile on her lips.

Cooper pushed the front door open. "When I entered the anteroom by the vault, I spotted three men wearing gorilla masks. Two guards lay on the floor in their underwear. One of the men shouted at me to lay on the floor or he'd shoot. It was Carl."

I glanced at him as we stepped outside. "How could you tell behind that mask?"

"His size, his voice. I'd recognize it anywhere. And his suit. It was herringbone. I'd commented on it that morning. He shouted at me again to lie down, but I was so flustered, I just stood there." He laid his hand on his left side. "He came right up in front of me and jabbed the gun in my side. He was wearing gloves. I tried to reason with him, and that's when he shot me. I fell to the floor and played dead."

I paused at my pickup. "You were lucky it didn't hit anything vital."

He chuckled. "Tell me about it."

"Any idea where he might have run? I mean, in all the years you two knew each other, he must have mentioned someplace he wanted to visit."

Cooper paused, thoughtfully twisting the wedding band on his finger as he pondered his answer. He shook his head. "Not really."

I remembered the fishing trip Carl had told me about. "He ever say anything to you about Lake Falcon, about retiring down there?"

He shrugged. "Not that I remember."

Prompting him, I said. "Nothing about fishing or anything like that?"

"Nope." He eyed me warily, which nagged at me for a few moments, but I shrugged it off. He continued, "You and Carl were good friends, huh?"

I opened the pickup door. "I wouldn't say that. We were just acquaintances. We had lunch from time to time." I paused and chuckled. "Gave both of us the chance to get our jobs off our chests." I shook my head. "It's still hard for me to believe. I never saw the man when he wasn't upbeat—except once, around the end of January," I added, remembering that day at the deli when he was concerned over some problems, at work I'd guessed.

Cooper lifted an eyebrow. "You're kidding. I never saw him upset about anything."

I rolled down the window and climbed in, slamming the door behind me. "He was that day. He was worried about something. I just figured the credit union. Maybe not."

For a moment, I thought I saw a dark cloud flicker over Cooper's eyes, but he grinned and laughed. "I bet he told you some wild stories about his job, huh?" Before I could reply, he added, "It gets crazy down here at times."

I laughed. "I bet it does."

"You know," he continued, eyeing me curiously. "Now that I think about it, he talked a lot about England. Maybe that's where he is."

I shrugged. "Maybe." It wasn't but I didn't tell him so. Why would a man commit a half-million-dollar heist just to go to a country where he had already made arrangements to vacation during the Christmas holidays? I changed the subject. "I heard that the equipment videoing the transfer had been turned off."

A wry grin tugged at his lips. "Carl didn't miss a beat. That's something I wouldn't have thought of."

I frowned. "Was the video in a locked room or what?"

He shook his head. "No. We have it in the employee lounge."

I wanted to say "So anyone could have turned it off," but instead, I just nodded.

As I drove away, I told myself that something didn't fit, but I had no idea what. None of what I had learned suggested Carl Edwards was a thief, yet all of the evidence pointed to that very assumption.

Evidence, I reminded myself, never lies. It just sits there, waiting to be discovered, analyzed, and interpreted. I couldn't help thinking that in regard to Carl Edwards, either not all of the evidence had been gathered, or if it had, it had been interpreted inaccurately.

I glanced at my watch. Just after 12:00. I had a couple of hours to spare before showing up at the Edwards', so I decided to drop by downtown and see what I could find out about my old man's situation.

During the drive to Sixth Street, I went over my conversation with Frank Cooper. His description of Carl Edwards piqued my curiosity. Edwards was a slight man, about four or five inches shorter than me, which would make him around five feet six. He was wearing a herringbone suit and gloves. Of course, any experienced hood wears gloves as a precaution against leaving prints. In addition to guarding against leaving prints, however, gloves could also prevent identification of gender.

I grimaced and flexed my fingers on the steering wheel of my Silverado pickup. Wouldn't it be something if a woman pulled it off and Carl Edwards was nailed for it?

Stranger things have happened in the world of American jurisprudence.

Of course, Cooper's description put Raiford Lindsey out of the picture. Lindsey was well over six feet in both directions.

Sixth Street is Austin's answer to New Orleans' French Quarter, although even the most passionate Austinite would have to admit the street lacks the charm of the quarter. Still, it can match the rowdiness and bizarre behavior of The City That Care Forgot.

Over the years, I'd developed a cadre of winos who often furnished me with information I'd not have been able to secure elsewhere. I first met them years back through my old man, whom I'd found in one of the alleyways behind Sixth Street. While the transient population was in a constant state of flux as new ones came in and old ones left, a few remained, Goofyfoot and Downtown, to name a couple.

I spotted a wizened old man in baggy clothes near the convention center. I pulled to the curb and honked.

The old man jerked to a halt when he saw me waving to him and immediately turned back in the direction from which he had come.

I shouted, "Hey, Goofyfoot. It's me, Tony, Tony Boudreaux."

He paused and looked around, peering at me skeptically with his watery blue eyes. "Boudreaux?" He took a hesitant step toward me, his baggy coat dragging the ground beside his ragged running shoes.

"Yeah. It's me."

He shuffled up to the pickup, his pigeon-toed foot twisted in at almost a thirty-degree angle. The rubber sole outside his little toe was worn away.

Leaning out the window, I gestured down the alley. "Where's all the boys?"

He grew serious. "They be around." His eyes narrowed. "Looking for somebody?"

"Yep. You remember my old man?" Goofyfoot frowned. I continued, "He's in town."

He shook his head. "I ain't seen him."

"I know. He's at my place. Seems like he had a few problems down at the rail yard a couple nights back. Some guy by the name of Salinas Sal got himself killed. Is there anything on the street about it?"

His eyes took on a shifty look. "Might be."

I chuckled and handed him a sawbuck. He hastily stuffed it into the wrinkles of the baggy clothes hanging from his bony frame. "I don't know for sure, but a new boy come in. Calls hisself Butcherman. I ain't seen him, but Downtown said this one, he was looking to hide out. Said he'd seen a dude wasted and the killers came after him."

My hopes surged. "Did he say where?" Goofyfoot shook his head, and I continued, "This Butcherman—think you can find him for me? No cops involved. Just him and me anywhere he wants. It's worth a hundred bucks."

Goofyfoot's eyes grew wide, and then quickly narrowed. I knew exactly what the shrewd little grifter had in mind, but I didn't care as long as I could talk to Butcherman. "Let me see what I can do."

I winked at him. "I'll be around tonight. Down at Neon Larry's."

Chapter Eight

The Edwards lived in a steeply gabled Victorian two-story overlooking a five-acre lake in the middle of the fashionable gated community of Brentwood Estates west of Austin. I had a few questions I wanted to ask, but only of Debbie and her mother.

Debbie met me at the door, a wan smile on her drawn face. "Hi, Tony. Glad you could make it. Come on in."

The large house was tastefully decorated. In the den, bookcases lined one wall. An entertainment center took up most of a second wall, a fireplace the third, and an expanse of French doors on the fourth overlooked the lake below.

Mrs. Edwards came to meet me, her hand extended. "Thank you for coming." She turned to a woman on the couch. "This is Dorothy Winkler, the noted psychic."

I sensed a tension in the air.

Winkler rose and offered me her hand. A slight woman, she wore flowing white robes, and her jet-black hair hung to her waist. "Mr. Boudreaux."

Mrs. Edwards gestured to several personal items on the coffee table in front of the couch, among which was some fly-fishing tackle. She continued, "These are Carl's. That's how Dorothy establishes communication with him."

Mentally, I rolled my eyes.

Dorothy Winkler smiled at me, a dimple in each of her

cheeks and a mischievous gleam in her eyes. "I have the feeling you don't believe in psychics, Mr. Boudreaux."

I shrugged. "Call me Tony. Truth is, I don't know if I do or not. I guess I am skeptical, but I do know there is much in our world of which we are not aware." I grinned at Debbie and her mother. "I can tell you one thing though. There were times I thought my mother was psychic."

They all laughed, and the tension was broken, at least on their part. I was still skeptical.

She cleared her throat. "As I explained to Mrs. Edwards and Debbie, the word *psychic* refers to the ability to perceive things through means of extrasensory perception that is hidden from traditional senses." She paused with a shrug. "So, how does it work?" She chuckled and added, "I have no idea. As a child I didn't know I had a gift. I thought everyone could do as I could. Over the years, I've been able to assist many deserving families."

Debbie spoke up. "Dorothy has written several books. Some of them are best sellers."

I nodded. "I've seen them."

The slight psychic studied me another moment, and then drew a deep breath. "Shall we begin?" she asked Margaret Edwards.

We sat on the couch as Dorothy Winkler picked up a pair of cuff links and, closing her eyes, ran her fingers lightly over them for several moments.

Over the next few minutes, she did the same with articles of clothing, books, and even the fishing tackle. The soft features of her face grew hard and taut with stress. I didn't know if she were faking or truly enduring the agonies of psychokinesis.

Perspiration popped out on her forehead.

Debbie and I exchanged puzzled looks at the transition

that seemed to be taking place within the woman. Skeptical or not, I was growing alarmed.

After several minutes, she stiffened, drew a deep breath, and then allowed her shoulders to slump. Her eyes opened and, with an expression of relief, she sagged into the over-stuffed chair at the end of the couch, laid her head back, and closed her eyes once again.

We all leaned forward expectantly, and yes, while I wasn't convinced, I was curious as to the results.

Mrs. Edwards whispered, "Did you see him?"

Winkler's eyes fluttered. "I saw rocks and trees and something red."

Debbie exclaimed, "Dad's car. His Impala. It's red." She looked at her mother hopefully.

Her mother ignored her. "Is—Is he alive?" Her voice was merely a croak.

The slight woman rolled her head to the side so she could see Mrs. Edwards. "I don't know."

I spoke up. "Any hint of where the red object is?"

She furrowed her brow in concentration. "The rocks were white, and the red object was a great distance away, below me. Perhaps at the bottom of a canyon or hill. And," she added, "I saw water and floating on the water was a gold and silver wristwatch. There are no numbers on the face, no slashes, only dots." She paused, and then added, "Green dots."

Mrs. Edwards gasped and pressed her hands to her lips. Tears filled her eyes. "I gave Carl a watch like that for his birthday. It's in May, and emerald is his birthstone. Those are the green dots."

I glanced at the coffee table, but there was no watch. I stared at Dorothy Winkler in disbelief. How could she know that? Maybe Mrs. Edwards had mentioned a watch. On the other hand, I told myself, probably fifty percent of men's wristwatches are silver and gold. But how many of them use emeralds instead of numbers or slashes?

While Winkler regained her strength, Debbie walked out to the pickup with me. I still had a couple of questions on my mind, but I decided to wait until I was alone with Debbie and her mother.

I asked her if her mother had mentioned the watch to Winkler. "No. I was with Mother when Dorothy arrived. I never left the room." She paused, her forehead crumpled in a frown. "What do you think we should do now, Tony?"

"I haven't made any headway yet. Best thing to do is to tell the cops."

Her frown deepened. "What do we tell them?"

"I'll do it. I'll tell them we talked to a psychic, and we're looking for a red Impala at the bottom of a canyon that has a creek running through it." I couldn't believe it was me talking, but then, I reminded myself, it was the only lead we had.

I had expected Chief Ramon Pachuca to throw me out of his office when I told him about our session with the psychic, but to my surprise, he nodded. "Dorothy Winkler? Sure, I know the woman. We've used her a few times. Some of the stuff she sees, or however she does it, is downright uncanny." He paused and chuckled. "Some isn't, but it's worth a shot." He picked up the phone. "Wilson. I'm sending Boudreaux out there. Take his information and put it out to all cruisers. Oh, and send it to the Sheriff's office too. His constables can help us search. Get them off their fat keisters."

*   *   *

By the time I climbed into my pickup, it was almost 5:00. I headed back to the credit union. I wanted to visit with Judith Perry, but away from her work environment. Just how to approach her, I wasn't quite sure.

I almost missed her. As I pulled into the credit union parking lot, I spotted her climb into a new Mustang, slam the door, and leave two black stripes of rubber on the parking lot as she shot into the traffic. I did my best not to lose sight of her, but weaving from one lane to another, she quickly vanished. I followed, uncertain as to my next step.

To my delight, she made up my mind for me when a few minutes later, she pulled into the Bo Peep Lounge perched on the limestone bluffs overlooking the Colorado River a hundred feet below.

I spotted the Mustang as I passed. Quickly, I made a U-turn and headed back. Just as I signaled to turn across the oncoming traffic, a tan Honda pulled up next to the Mustang, and a bright and sunny blond bounced out. Judith climbed out to meet her, gesticulating wildly. The blond tried to pacify her. By the time I found a parking spot, the two had disappeared into the lounge.

I paused just inside the door to accustom my eyes to the dim lighting. The Bo Peep was an upscale lounge, catering to the upwardly mobile within the community. There were half a dozen couples in the lounge, some at the bar, some at the tables around the dance floor, and another couple shooting pool at a corner table. I spotted Perry and her friend in a booth along one wall.

With my back to them, I slipped into the next booth and ordered a beer.

I got lucky. Perry was furious. She and Busby had a spat

earlier when he informed her their relationship had run its course.

Some of her ensuing comments would bruise the ears of the less sophisticated. For the next few minutes, I listened as two avant-garde women neatly dissected the male species' ancestral background with visceral efficiency.

I glanced around the lounge, spotting a couple of single males, both casting lecherous glances at the two women. I grinned to myself, wondering if I should hang around and watch the fireworks when one of them garnered the nerve to ask one of the ladies to dance.

Pushing the beer away, I rose and headed for the door. Now was not the time to speak with Judith Perry.

Outside, I jotted down her license, and ten minutes later had her address and phone number. I drove by her place, a condo in the Silvercreek Manor Complex. I arched an eyebrow, impressed. "Not bad," I muttered. "Not bad at all." I'd check with her later that night after I changed clothes and came up with a pretext that would cause her to spill everything she knew about Marvin Busby.

Chapter Nine

The sun had dropped behind the skyline of downtown Austin by the time I hit Sixth Street. I parked in the alley behind Neon Larry's Bar and Grill. Larry and I go way back, and I often used his back door as a shortcut to Sixth Street.

I waved as I passed the bar. "Seen Goofyfoot around? I was supposed to meet him out front."

The lean man shook his head. "How about a beer?" he called out above the steady rumble of the crowd.

"Maybe later."

Outside, I looked up and down the street. Tourists, drunks, college kids, and the simply curious were beginning to fill the sidewalks. Soon several blocks of the street would be one big party punctuated by angry confrontations, annoyed cops, and acerbic curses until around two in the morning.

I headed down the sidewalk. As I approached Neches Street, I spotted Goofyfoot. He saw me at the same time, and hurriedly shuffled toward me. "You find him?"

The wizened old man nodded. "Where's the hundred?"

"What hundred?" I tried not to grin.

He studied me a moment. "For the Butcherman."

"I'll give it to him when I see him."

Goofyfoot pressed his cracked lips together.

I laughed. "What are you trying to do, con him out of half of it?"

He frowned. "It ought to be worth something to me for finding him for you."

"I gave you a sawbuck this morning."

His frown deepened.

"All right. Another ten. Satisfied?" I patted my pocket. "The hundred I give to him."

Goofyfoot agreed. The old man would have gone along with five bucks or less, but every time I saw him or any of the other transients, I thought of my old man and hoped that wherever he was at that moment, someone would lend him a hand if he needed it.

He grabbed the ten and stuck it into the tangle of rags hanging off him. "In the alley up there," he said, nodding to the alley north of Sixth Street.

He started to walk away, but I stopped him. "No, you don't. Show me."

Like every alley in downtown Austin, this one was lined with Dumpsters overflowing with trash. Next to some of the Dumpsters were cardboard boxes that transients called home sweet home.

We found the Butcherman curled inside a cardboard box beside the Dumpster that served Wichie's Last Chance Bar. Enraged, he came boiling out when Goofyfoot kicked the box.

Fists doubled and his face twisted in anger, he shouted, "What do you think you're doing?" Short and stocky, Butcherman wore jeans and a denim jacket. His western hat was soiled, but the brim still maintained its rakish curves. He didn't look like one of the archetypal transients. On the other hand, maybe he was new to the business. When he recognized Goofyfoot, his anger faded.

Goofyfoot looked up at me. "This is him."

Butcherman studied me, and then held out his hand to Goofyfoot. "Where's my forty?"

I looked down at Goofyfoot. "Why, you two-timing little sneak. I—"

"Can't blame a guy for trying, can you?" He turned and quickly shuffled away.

Butcherman yelled after him, but I held up my hand. "I've got your money. A hundred bucks."

He stared at me in disbelief for a moment, and then his eyes blazed as he glared after Goofyfoot. "A hundred? Why that—"

"Forget about him. I've got a couple questions, and then the money's yours." I hooked my thumb at Wichie's. "How about a drink?"

He pulled out a pack of crumpled cigarettes and touched a match to one. "Sure."

Inside, we sat near the hall leading out the back. He ordered a double bourbon neat. I ordered a cup of coffee.

"Goofyfoot said you saw a dude wasted." He sipped his bourbon and just stared at me. I recognized the animal wariness in his eyes. "I'm not a cop. My old man has been accused of killing that guy. The dead guy's name, by the way, was Salinas Sal. I'm just trying to get a lead on who did the job."

He studied me another moment, downed his bourbon, and ordered another double. Lighting up another cigarette, he replied in a raspy voice, "Yeah, I knew Sal. I know your old man too. Boudreaux? Some kind of Frenchy?"

I nodded. "Go on."

"We got in from San Antone. I hopped off. Sal figured on staying in the car, but then he decided he'd come down here and pick up a few bucks before heading on to Fort Worth."

"What about my old man? What did he do?"

"Nothing. I think he was passed out somewhere. I ain't sure. Anyway, I worked the streets until about two or three, and then headed back to the rail yard. I'd spotted a snug hole to bunk in. When I got close, I saw two men bending over someone on the ground. I was in the streetlight, and they spotted me. One of them yelled for me to come over, but I took off running. I ditched them and hid out in a culvert all night. I didn't know the dude on the ground was Sal until next morning when I heard it on the street." He shook his head. "They'd of killed me too."

"What did they look like? Can you describe them?"

He grimaced. "Tall. About like you. One a couple of inches shorter. His face was all marked up." He jabbed his finger at his cheeks. "What do you call that stuff that scars up people's faces?"

"Acne?"

He nodded emphatically. "Yeah. Acne. Real bad scars."

By now, he was on his third double.

"Any idea why they wasted him?"

He stubbed out his cigarette. "I ain't sure, but I figure it might have something to do about the time Sal stumbled onto some old boys dumping a body in the back of a car. They was probably them old boys."

"When was that?"

He shrugged. "Oh, some weeks back. That's why he left town and went to San Antone."

"San Antone, huh?"

"Yep, according to what he said, he was out at Barton Springs—you know, the swimming hole. Two cars drove up. That's what woke him. He was sleeping under a picnic table. He laid there and watched when they pulled the body out of a big car and dumped it in the trunk of another one." He fumbled in his shirt pocket and pulled out an empty pack of cigarettes. He looked up at me. He had me right where he wanted me, that little sucker.

I held up the empty cigarette package to the bartender. Moments later, Butcherman lit up again.

"So, then what?"

"They spotted him, but he ditched them in the dark, but they was close enough that he heard one say he'd recognized Sal from Sixth Street. Sal lost no time in grabbing a freight for San Antone."

At least I was getting close. If I could manage to learn the identity of one of the two goombahs, then maybe that would help get my old man off the hook.

Butcherman started to push back from the table. "I've got to get another pack of smokes before I leave. It's a long ride to Fort Worth."

"Hold on," I said. "I'll get them. You've done me a big favor."

As I stood at the bar, I heard the front door slam open. I glanced around to see two dudes, one with an acne-scarred face and wearing a black leather jacket, charging across the room toward Butcherman. All I glimpsed of the second one was a red Windbreaker.

Butcherman darted out the back.

Before I could say a word, Acne Face plowed into a customer who slammed back into me, spinning me around and smacking my forehead into the bar.

My head exploded and, for a moment, I fought against a wave of dizziness.

I must have lost the battle, for the next thing I knew I was staring up into the grim face of a paramedic who was tending the hen egg on my forehead just above my eye. He lifted an eyebrow. "Split the skin, buddy, but not bad. Band-Aid will take care of it."

After another few moments making sure my brain wasn't scrambled, hands helped me off the floor into a chair. A cold glass of water appeared before me. Not even an ice-cold beer ever tasted so good.

I tried to collect my thoughts, but they were tumbling about in my head like a bunch of crazed acrobats. And then the events of the last few minutes cut through the fog in my head. I looked around. "The guy I was with, the one wearing the denim jacket. Where'd he go?"

The bartender shrugged and pushed his long greasy hair back over his shoulders. "Out the back with them two right on his tail. I ran out there, but they was disappearing around the corner of the alley on Neches Street."

I tried to rise, but my legs grew shaky. Hands guided me back down into my chair. "Take it easy, pal. You need a ride home?"

"No," I muttered. "Just let me sit here a few minutes. I'll be all right."

I hoped.

Chapter Ten

During the drive home, I tried to sort my thoughts, but all I remembered about the two thugs was that Acne Face wore a black leather jacket, and the second one a red Windbreaker.

My head was pounding when I pulled into the driveway at my apartment. A relaxing shower and a clean change of clothes would make me feel better. But I hadn't counted on my old man.

He was up and about, ticked off because I'd been gone all day and all he had to eat was frozen pizzas. I snapped at him, "Well, you had beer, didn't you?"

He snorted. "You can't live on beer." He eyed my black eye and swollen forehead.

I rolled my eyes. That remark from a drunk who'd lived on nothing but beer and wine for at least thirty years. I studied him, once again asking myself just how his bone-thin body survived the ravages of alcohol for all those years. Based on every twenty-million-dollar report I'd seen from various governmental agencies, he should have been dead twenty years ago.

On the other hand, the truth was probably closer to an observation made by my doctor that booze won't kill you, but it will embalm you and leave you a walking mummy. In other words, if it doesn't kill you, it'll pickle your brain.

I glanced at the clock. Almost 8:00. If I were going to see Judith Perry, I didn't have any time to waste. "All right. I'll pick up some frozen dinners. What do you like, beef, chicken, turkey, what?"

He shrugged. "No difference as long as it ain't pizza."

"I'll bring it as soon as I finish my appointment."

He glared at me. "What am I supposed to do until then if I can't leave this dump?"

I bristled at his remark, but I held my temper. "Well, then, John Roney, I suppose you'll just have to starve."

"Not me." He shook his head and eyed me defiantly. "I'm going out to get me a hamburger and a bottle of wine."

I clenched my teeth. "You do, I promise you, you'll spend the night in jail, and I won't get you out until your trial." I paused and for good measure, added, "And don't expect me to post your bail a second time."

I stormed into the bathroom and slammed the door. I grimaced when I looked in the mirror. I had a good-sized knot covered by a Band-Aid over my left eye, which was almost black. "At least," I muttered, "Perry won't recognize me." Hey, I almost didn't recognize myself.

Contrary to my hopes, I didn't feel any better after my shower. My head still pounded. Ignoring my old man, I went into the kitchen and downed a couple of Excedrin. I jabbed a finger at him before I left. "I'll be gone a couple of hours. Don't step outside this door." I glared at him, and he glared back.

I swung by the Bo Peep Lounge. Perry's Mustang was gone. I crossed my fingers that she was home.

To my delight, her Mustang was in its parking spot. I checked myself out in the rearview mirror. Even without the knot on my head, I presented a different image from my casual dress that morning. A business suit, white shirt, and tie make a world of difference.

In the PI business, often we resort to pretext, which is a politically correct term for lying. It's a sneaky business at times, and that's when you have to use sneaky means to gather information.

I have four or five identities, all of which I have used at one time or another over the last several years. For each, I have a driver's license, business cards, all the accoutrements essential in convincing a mark of my occupation.

My identities included PIs, salesmen, meter readers, cab drivers, and even a minister. Tonight, I opted for the PI.

Just after 9:00, I rang her doorbell. I could hear the TV inside. I stood in front of the peephole in the door. Moments later, the door opened a crack and a pair of eyes looked out. A wary voice said, "Yes?"

I stepped back a couple of paces, giving assurance that I wasn't about to throw a shoulder into the door. "Sorry to bother you, miss, but I'm looking for Judith Perry of Tri-District Credit Union." I extended my arm, offering a business card through the crack between the door and jamb. "My name is Mort Tavin. I'm a private investigator. I've been hired by a law firm out of Dallas to inquire into the activities of a Mr. Marvin Busby." I paused and indicated the knot on my head. "I know I look like something from a bad movie, but to tell the truth, I ran into a door at the motel."

She took the card, scanned it, and then muttered through the crack. "I don't understand. What activities?"

Glancing up and down the gallery, I replied, "I would prefer to come in, but if you're concerned about your safety, we can meet tomorrow." I handed her my driver's license and a copy of my PI license. "Perhaps these will ease your anxieties about me."

She looked the licenses over and then closed the door. I heard the safety chain being removed, and the door opened. "Please, come in, Mr. Tavin." She returned the licenses and gestured to a chair at the end of a couch.

Except for removing the billowing pink bow about her neck, she had not changed from her work clothes, slacks and a lacy pink blouse. She nodded to a half-full glass on the coffee table. "I was having a drink. Care to join me?"

"No, thanks," I replied with a bright smile. "I know it's late, but I have a sick child back in Dallas, and you're my last person to interview. I plan to drive back tonight." As long as I was laying a lie on her, I figured I might as well lay it on thick.

"I'm sorry," she replied, sitting on the edge of the couch and crossing her legs. "Serious?"

"Our first. Everything is serious with that one."

She frowned, for I knew she could tell at a glance I was not one of those proverbial spring chickens.

"I married late," I explained. "So naturally, I'm sometimes overly concerned about the little girl."

Judith leaned forward, her square face framed by soft brown hair. Somehow her regular features glittered with a charming beauty. "I hope she's okay."

"Thank you." I pulled out a notepad on which I had jotted a couple of questions. "Now, about Marvin Busby. One of my sources, and I'm sorry, but you understand by law, I cannot identify them, suggested you and Busby were long-time acquaintances."

She leaned back slightly, suggesting a wariness of the direction questioning might take. "Yes. We've worked together for many years."

"Fine. Now, there are a couple of issues I've been hired

to look into. First, his financial status. Do you know if he has any problems in that regard?"

She shrugged, and I could see her brain whirling. "Probably no more than most of us."

"Now, he's divorced, and—"

"Certainly. I would never go out with a married man."

I lifted an eyebrow. "Oh, you and Mr. Busby have dated?"

A faint grimace flickered across her face. "A couple times."

I shrugged. "No matter." I glanced at the notepad.

"Tell me," she said, interrupting. "What is this all about? What is Marvin supposed to be guilty of?"

Then I dropped the bombshell as gently as I could. "Well, I guess I can mention it. There have been a couple of accusations of paternity." Her eyes grew wide. I hastily continued. "But I have found no evidence of it." I paused, and then casually added, "Although I do have a few more individuals to interview in another city."

She stammered a moment. "Paternity! You mean—"

I held up my hand. "I don't know. All I know is accusations, according to his lawyer, have been made, but—" I hesitated, giving the impression I was wrestling with my conscience, and then added, "I shouldn't say this, but so far I've found nothing to support it."

"Paternity!" If the word could be spat out, she spat it out. "Why, that—" She turned up her bourbon and downed it. She glared at me, her face turning various shades of red. "Let me tell you about Marvin Busby. He's a no-good, two-timing jerk. Why, I wouldn't be surprised if he wasn't also accused of bigamy."

I knew I would hate myself the next morning, but I couldn't resist. "Well, I wasn't going to mention that, but—"

She stared at me in disbelief. "You—You mean—"

I nodded and held up two fingers.

All she could do was sputter.

"Naturally, the plaintiffs are demanding support, and if their accusations are true, which I don't know, then—"

"Then they should have it," she blurted out. She grabbed the bourbon bottle and splashed several ounces into her glass. She held the bottle out to me, but I declined. Her eyes blazed. "Let me tell you about Marvin. He's been going through the change of life for the last ten years. He fancies himself a playboy and gambler. Five or six times a month, he heads to casinos out of state. I don't know how much he owes, but his credit cards are maxed. He's into me for almost twenty thousand, and now it looks like he's latched onto some other fool." She downed a couple of gulps and then, very unladylike, wiped her lips with the back of her hand, smearing her lipstick. "And I'll bet if you check with his ex-wife, he hasn't paid her any support in years."

Nodding while I jotted on my notepad, I asked. "Would you happen to remember any of the casinos he visited?"

She hesitated a moment, pursing her lips. "Well, there was Harrah's in New Orleans, the Thunderbird in Santa Rosa, New Mexico, and the Star Shine in Las Vegas."

From all she had told me, I figured Marvin Busby was one fairly solid suspect. He had motive and, if he were at work that day, he had opportunity. I wanted to ask her about Carl Edwards, but I was afraid she might begin to wonder what he had to do with Busby's problems.

Maybe I could finesse some information from her. I closed my notepad and slipped it in my pocket. "I guess that's about it." I stared at the ceiling. "Tri-District Credit Union. Seems like I heard something about it a few weeks ago."

She arched an eyebrow. "You did. We were robbed of half a million dollars."

"That's it." I nodded. "I knew I'd heard something. They catch the thieves?"

By now her eyes were getting glassy. "No. Not the money either."

"They got any ideas?"

"Yeah. They think the first vice president, Carl Edwards, did it." She chewed on her bottom lip, and then added in a slur, "But I don't think he did."

"Oh, why not?"

She emphasized the reason by jabbing the glass of bourbon at me. "Decent guy. He didn't need the money. Personally, a louse like Marvin Busby would be more likely to do something like that."

In wide-eyed innocence, I asked, "Was Busby at work that day? I mean the day of the robbery?"

Either my question or the bourbon confused her. "Yeah, yeah. Marvin—at least one thing I can say for that snake is that he never misses work. Gets a kick out of turning down loans."

I pushed to my feet and extended my hand. "You've given me more than enough, Miss Perry. Thank you very much."

Sitting in my pickup, I stared up at her porch light. Now I had to find out just how deep in debt Busby was. Surely Danny knew the proprietors of the three casinos. I glanced at my watch: 10:30. He'd still be awake.

He was, but he was out. "No problem." I handed his soldier a note. "Give this to him for me, if you don't mind."

* * *

After leaving Danny's parking garage, I wove through downtown toward the interstate. At the corner of Third and Red River, I spotted a couple of cruisers with their overheads flashing and an ambulance. I started to drive past, but I recognized one of the officers. I pulled over and rolled down the window. "Hey, Wehring. What's up?"

He peered at me for several moments before he recognized me. "Boudreaux! That you?" He ambled over to the pickup. He grinned at my black eye. "Looks like you got the short of it, huh?"

"Yeah." I nodded to the ambulance. "Earning your money tonight, huh?"

He chuckled. "Not really. Just another one of those winos. Been in that Dumpster a day or so. Someone beat him up good. Must've used a ball bat."

"One of our locals?"

"Nah. Never saw him around. A cowboy type."

My blood ran cold. "Cowboy?"

"Yeah, you know. Black cowboy hat, a denim jacket, jeans."

Butcherman!

Those two goons had caught up with him, the same two he'd spotted at the rail yard bending over the dead wino.

Chapter Eleven

Next morning on the way to the credit union, I swung by the Green Light Parking Garage, a seven-story edifice west of the convention center.

As always, one of Danny's soldiers stood at the elevator doors at the first floor. I asked to see Danny. He called upstairs and, moments later, nodded and the elevator doors hissed open.

Danny was sitting at a glass-topped table sipping coffee and slicing into a couple of pieces of French toast soaked with maple syrup. He wore a royal purple dressing robe with a black velvet collar. He whistled when he spotted my black eye. "Jeez. What happened to you? Come on over and have some breakfast."

I declined. "I'll take some coffee." I touched the knot on my forehead. "I forgot to duck."

He laughed. "I bet."

I glanced at my watch. "Yep."

He shrugged and poked a bite in his mouth. While he was chewing, he announced, "I haven't looked into the casino business yet. I'll take care of it later this morning."

"Great, and I need another favor. I'm looking for a bozo with an acne-scarred face. About my height."

"New in town or what?"

I sipped my coffee. "I don't know."

"Something to do with the credit union?"

"No. He might have something to do with a dead wino a couple days back."

Danny frowned up at me. "Wino?"

"Cops think my old man might have done it."

"Oh." He nodded his understanding. He glanced at the soldier standing by the door and snapped his fingers. With a short nod, the nattily dressed buttonman stepped into the elevator. "I'll see what I can find out. Give me a call about noon. I'll know something about this Busby dude too," Danny said. "Now, you sure you don't want some French toast?"

I glanced at my watch. I had a few minutes to spare. "Why not?"

To my relief, Judith Perry was not at her teller window when I pushed through the doors of the credit union. I hurried to the conference room and waited for my first interviews.

All the information I had about Mary Louise Smith was that she was a longtime dog and pony fan, and that a few weeks earlier, she had settled a fifteen-thousand-dollar obligation to Pete Garza at the Juarez dog track.

She paused at the open door. "Mr. Boudreaux?" A petite woman in her mid-forties, she dressed ten years younger, and it was obvious she was meticulous in her overall appearance.

She wore a green, what most would call lime, pantsuit and a plain white blouse with a button collar and a gold necktie. She didn't look like a racetrack aficionado, but then, no one does, for they come from every cultural and economic arena.

I rose quickly. "Ms. Smith. Thank you for coming."

She eyed my black eye suspiciously. "I didn't have a choice. Mr. Lindsey made sure of that."

It didn't take the *Psychology for Dummies* book to tell she was hostile. I gestured to a chair across the long table. "Please have a seat. This won't take long. All I need is a little information."

"About Carl Edwards?" Her tone was defiant.

"Look, we all know he's believed to have been behind the robbery. He's dropped out of sight. His wife and daughter hired me to find him." I shrugged. "That's all this is about." That was a white lie, for I wanted to do a little more digging than just that. I wasn't sure what I was looking for, perhaps something to convince me Edwards was indeed innocent.

Reluctantly, she slipped into the chair. She held herself erect. Her short black hair fell just below her ears. She eyed me coolly, with wary disdain.

Her opinion of Edwards was the same as the others I had spoken with. She shook her head emphatically. "The only way I would believe Carl committed the holdup was if he told me so face-to-face."

"You worked with him a good while, huh?"

"Over twenty years."

Feigning puzzlement, I replied, "I heard many express the same feelings, but from what little I've heard about the robbery, he's the only who could have pulled it off." I hastened to add, "Like I say, all I've heard is idle talk."

To my delight, the frozen expression of disdain on her face turned into a faint sneer. "Personally, I think you'd be wrong. But as far as I know, Carl might have done it. Or maybe Frank—or even Raiford. Not that I think either one did," she added.

"Frank? You mean Cooper? But he was shot. Edwards shot him."

Her tone became testy. "Look, Mr. Boudreaux. You asked what I thought. That's what I think." She shook her head. "As far as I'm concerned, Carl Edwards did it. I don't care as long as I keep getting my paycheck."

I grinned. "I don't blame you." I glanced at my notes. "Cooper said the head teller was responsible for checking in the weekly armored car delivery, but on that day Edwards told her he'd check in the delivery."

She shrugged. "No big deal. Sometimes if the teller wasn't available, Edwards or Cooper or one of the loan officers would take care of it."

"Loan officers?" I arched an eyebrow. "You're a loan officer, right?"

Her eyes narrowed. "Yes."

"Have you ever checked in the delivery?"

Her jaw stiffened. "What does that have to do with Carl Edwards?"

I watched her carefully, not wanting to miss any significant body language. For a moment, I hesitated, knowing my next remark would put me on dangerous ground with Chief Pachuca. Offhandedly, I replied, "Well, it's always prudent to find those who have motives for a crime and, to be honest, Ms. Smith. I know for a fact that three weeks ago, just a few days after the armored car heist, you paid off a fifteen-thousand-dollar debt to Pete Garza down at Juarez."

If I'd hit her in the face with a coconut cream pie, she couldn't have been any more stunned. Her eyes grew wide, and her jaw dropped. She gaped at me for several seconds, before managing to stammer. "H-How—"

In a patronizing tone, I replied, "Not that I think you had anything to do with it, but if you could answer my questions, it might help me see this whole situation a little more clearly."

Clearly bewildered, she sputtered, "But what can I tell you? I had nothing to do with it. I wasn't even at work that day. Besides, Frank Cooper said it was Carl who shot him. Why would he lie?"

I studied her. Either she was telling the truth, or she was an accomplished liar. "Frank Cooper didn't really see Edwards." She parted her lips to disagree, but I continued. "He saw someone wearing a gorilla mask, a herringbone suit, and gloves. Stop and think about it a moment. Edwards was a small man. A woman wearing the mask and his suit might pass themselves off as Edwards, especially wearing gloves to cover their hands."

Mary Louise stared at me, dumbfounded.

"Now, have you ever checked in the armored car delivery?"

She nodded woodenly. "Several times. Like I said, if the head teller was tied up, Carl or Frank or one of the loan officers did it."

"You mean Rita Johnson or Marvin Busby."

"Yes, and sometimes Larry Athens. He's vice president of Finance."

I cleared my throat. "Do you mind telling me where you were that day?"

She shook her head emphatically, her eyes glancing around nervously. "You're not going to believe it."

"Try me."

"I was in Juarez, at the track."

"By yourself?"

She hesitated. Slowly she nodded.

I prodded her. "Anyone see you there—anyone who could vouch for you? What about Pete Garza?"

She dropped her gaze to the table, and then looked up at me, her eyes pleading. "No. No one. But I'm telling the truth. I was there." She paused, and then added enthusiastically, "I still have the stubs from the races."

"One more question, Ms. Smith. Any idea who turned the video off that day?"

She frowned. "I didn't know it was off."

"It was."

With a shrug, she replied, "Could have been anyone. The monitor and recorder are in the employee lounge."

So much for the video.

Take ten years off Mary Louise Smith and you had Rita Johnson. Both ladies dressed professionally and carried themselves as such. Johnson was a tall woman and seemed proud of it, for she carried herself with regal demeanor.

As soon as I saw Rita Johnson, I started to discount her as pulling the heist. She was about my height, large-boned, but very graceful and feminine. Her auburn air came to just below her ears. Still, I told myself, staring down the muzzle of an automatic could have confused Frank Cooper. He could have been off a couple of inches in his estimate of the perp's height.

Graciously ignoring my black eye and the knot on my head, she was as pleasant as Mary Louise was curt. "Anything I can do to help, I will."

All I knew about her was her children were grown, and she and her husband were compulsive gamblers. From what I had learned, they were not in debt to anyone. As we spoke, I quickly discovered she felt like the others regarding Carl Edwards.

When I asked if she had any idea where he might have gone, she replied, "No. Oh, from time to time, he talked about fishing down at some place called Lake Falcon, but lately he'd talked about trout fishing up in the mountains in New Mexico."

I paused, turning the bit of information over in my head, remembering the fly-fishing tackle on the coffee table in the Edwards' living room. "New Mexico, huh? Did he ever make the trip?" I couldn't help wondering why he hadn't mentioned New Mexico to me that day he invited me to go on the Falcon trip.

She laughed, a bright animated chuckled. "I suppose so. You see, we weren't close friends, but I knew if I ever needed any help, Carl was always there. He was—" She hesitated, and her cheeks colored with a blush. "He is one of the nicest people I've ever known. Nice to everyone. I had some personal problems a while back, and he was very understanding." She laughed. "He always stopped by to say hi. I don't know. Maybe it was because we're both southpaws."

I laughed with her. "Did he ever give a name—you know—a resort that he wanted to visit in New Mexico?"

She hesitated, her forehead wrinkled in a frown. "Yes. There was someplace he had been before, but to be honest, I can't remember. I'm sorry."

"No problem." I held up a hand. "If you do, let me know." I handed her a card.

She studied the card. "Lost Lake. That's it," she exclaimed. "I just remembered. Lost Lake. That's where he wanted to visit. He said the trout fishing was fantastic up there."

After she left, I considered our conversation. Although the New Mexico mountains were probably still filled with snow, I couldn't afford to discount the idea he might have picked that spot to hide. While I was finding it more and more difficult to believe Edwards pulled the job, I still had to look at every possibility, turn over every stone, even if that meant a visit to Lost Lake.

It was almost noon when I took a break. I left by the side door, avoiding a possible run-in with Judith Perry. I paused before buckling up and called Danny, who insisted we have lunch out at the County Line Barbecue off Bee Tree Road.

I didn't argue. The County Line and its barbecue are world renowned. If not, they should be.

Chapter Twelve

Danny was his usual amiable self. With his red hair and freckled face, he reminded me of a mischievous leprechaun. During the drive to the restaurant, he regaled me with one joke after another.

I mentioned earlier that I'm not so naïve that I believe there's no gambling in Texas, with the exception of a few legal tracks and the Texas lottery and its spinoffs.

There are betting pots for everything and, in the subterranean world of big-time gambling, there are bookies who'll gladly take your money on everything from who hits the first triple in a ball game to which jockey spits on the ground first.

But, as we sat over a platter of juicy ribs, I wasn't prepared for the view that Danny opened for me.

"For your information, there are half a dozen "safe" casinos within thirty minutes of city limits. You name the game, and they have it: roulette, blackjack, craps—I could go on and on, but you get the idea. For a nice fee, chartered jets haul customers to Vegas, New Orleans, Lake Charles." He paused to tear a chunk of juicy pork from the rib bone he held delicately in his fingers. "You name it, we provide it."

A hundred questions bounced about in my head, but all I could manage was "That's hard to believe."

Danny chuckled. "Maybe so for straight arrows like you,

but not everyone is on the up and up." He jabbed the pork rib at the door. "You'd be surprised how many sinners live out there."

"You're telling me if I wanted to go to a casino around here, I wouldn't have any problem."

He laughed. "You bet you'd have a problem. The only way you get in is by referral. Most get it from legit casinos run by the same people who run the shady ones."

"How does that work?"

With a shrug, he replied, "Word of mouth. The house gets a regular player in there; they find out all about them. Over a period of time, they pass word to the suckers where they can find action closer to home." He took a bite of pork. "The marks like it because it saves them travel expenses, money they can sink in the slots or card games."

All I could say was "Live and learn."

Dabbing at the barbecue sauce on his lips, he replied, "Along those lines, I found out more about that Busby guy."

He went on to inform me that Marvin Busby, in addition to owing eight thousand to Frank Trimunti at a local game, had lost close to seventy thousand in the last six months.

I paused, barbecue sauce dripping from my chin, staring at Danny in disbelief. "Seventy thousand? How? And where?"

He laughed, the freckles on his face blending into a single red blotch. "There are ways. Any sucker bitten by the gambling bug will always find ways to lose money."

All I could do was shake my head and reach for another rib. "So, any luck on Acne Face?"

"Yep. Hymie Weinshank. Been around this part of the country a year or so, down from New Jersey. Does odd jobs for a price."

He didn't have to tell me what he meant by "odd jobs." "What about his partner?"

Pausing to swallow a bite of pork, Danny replied, "No one in particular. He hangs with Maury Erickson and Alex White down at the Zuider Zee on the river." He took a gulp of beer. "We've had no run-ins with them."

I parked the information in the back of my head. "Thanks." I'd worry later just how I would handle this last bit of news.

After I left Danny's parking garage, I pulled onto Sixth Street and headed for the Tri-District Credit Union. Behind me, overheads flashed. I pulled to the curb, puzzled. All my lights were working, and I hadn't run any signals. I rolled down the window. A uniform stepped up to the door. "Boudreaux? Tony Boudreaux?"

"Yeah." I nodded.

"Chief Pachuca wants to see you."

I didn't argue. "I'll go right over."

He grinned and touched a finger to his forehead.

Pachuca looked up from his desk when I entered, a frown knitting his brow. His dark eyes glanced at my forehead and black eye. "Boudreaux!"

"Chief."

I started to sit, but he barked, "Don't sit. You won't be here that long."

My pulse skipped a beat. I racked my brain trying to figure what I had done wrong. "What's up?"

"We got an anonymous call that you were sticking your nose in our business."

My mind raced. I fell back on that timeworn technique of deny, deny, deny. "I don't know what you mean, Chief."

He eyed me narrowly. "You haven't been suggesting to anyone out at the credit union that Carl Edwards was not the perpetrator of the armored car robbery?" He framed it as a question, but I knew it was an accusation.

I shook my head, my face beaming with innocence. "No. Not one word. You know how people are, Chief. Now, I'm not saying that someone might have misinterpreted what I asked, but all I tried to learn is if any of them had an idea where he might have gone." I paused. "You know I'd never do anything to cause problems for you, Chief. You've helped me too many times for me to jeopardize our working relationship."

He snorted. "We don't have a working relationship, Boudreaux. You do. And I'd better not find out you're lying to me, you hear?"

"I understand. Now, let me ask you something about the heist."

His eyes narrowed. "Like what?"

"Edwards' accomplices. Any lead on them?" I caught myself. "Sorry, I didn't mean that. What I meant was—"

He interrupted. "I know what you meant. We figure when we find Edwards, we'll find them. Now, are you satisfied? Anything else?"

I started to tell him what Butcherman had told me about Weinshank, Erickson, and White, thinking it would help my old man. Then I reminded myself I had no proof other than what I'd witnessed, and that was not sufficient to even warrant hauling in Weinshank or the others. "No, Chief. Nothing else. Nothing else at all, thanks."

Later, pushing aside the nagging feeling of guilt for not telling Pachuca about Weinshank and his partners, I sat in the pickup staring blankly at the brick and glass façade of the credit union as I tried to sort the disconnected ideas tumbling through my head.

Carl Edwards' motive for hitting the armored car was

weaker than a newborn kitten. There were half a dozen employees at the credit union who had more of a motive, although, according to Frank Cooper's story, only two of them might have passed for Edwards beneath the mask.

Rita Johnson was larger than Edwards, and from the glimpses I'd had of Busby and Athens, so were they.

Unless, I suddenly told myself, the stress and excitement of the robbery so confused Cooper that he saw what he wanted to see. Or hear, I reminded myself, remembering that he swore the voice behind the mask belonged to Edwards.

And then one of the lessons I learned from Al Grogan, our resident Sherlock Holmes back at Blevins' Security, kicked in. What if Cooper were not confused? What if he were lying?

Climbing from the pickup, I headed for the side door of the credit union, anxious to get the last two interviews over so I could get back to my computer to see what Eddie Dyson had found about Frank Cooper.

At about six feet two, Larry Athens was pushing sixty, but it was a trim sixty that many a thirty-year-old would envy. He paused at the door and threw up his hands when he spotted my black eye. "Whoa! Must've been a dandy fight."

I grinned. "Guess who lost."

A convivial man, he laughed and strode across the room. He shook my hand exuberantly and plopped down across the desk. "You've been asking about Carl, I hear." Before I could reply, he continued. "Nice guy." He went on to praise Edwards, just as all the others had, and to express his own surprise at hearing the news.

And no, Athens had no idea as to where he might have disappeared.

I probed. "None at all, huh? He never mentioned a trip, maybe a fishing trip? I hear he was an avid fly-fisherman."

The announcement surprised Athens. "I didn't know that. If I had, I would have taken Carl along with me on a couple of my trips back northeast. They got excellent trout fishing out there."

"Oh? You fly-fish?"

He shook his head and glanced over his shoulder. In a conspiratorial tone, he whispered, "I gamble." He paused for his announcement's effect on me. When he saw no reaction, he laughed and nodded in the direction of Raiford Lindsey's office. "Everybody here knows I gamble. That's my hobby. I'm divorced, no kids, and I like to gamble, so I go all over. Sometimes it's nice to have someone along just for the company. Old Carl could have fished while I gambled." He lifted an eyebrow and shrugged. "Might have been a good combination."

A frown knit my brows. "How's that?"

"I have a system," he announced. "I never gamble at night, only between ten and six. Those are my lucky hours. Never after dark. It's unlucky for me. In fact, after daylight savings time is over, some days I finish at five-thirty. Then I go to shows or something like that. It'd be nice to have someone to pal around with, you know?"

I nodded perfunctorily.

He grinned sheepishly at me. "To tell you the truth, I could have put that half million to good use." He roared with laughter.

I couldn't help smiling at his candor. "The day of the robbery. Did you see Edwards?"

His laughter faded as he concentrated. He grimaced. "I'd see him just about every day. Sometimes not. It's hard to remember."

"I think he had a bad cold that day."

His face lit. "Yeah. Now I remember. I tried to talk him into going home and climbing into bed, but he said he couldn't. He said—" He hesitated, his face growing grim. In a lowered voice, he continued, "He said he had an important job to do that day." He stared up at me, his eyes filled with sudden confusion. The slender man chewed on his bottom lip. "I still can't believe it."

While I didn't completely mark Larry Athens off my list, I put him close to the bottom, noting that once again, as with most of the others, he did not fit the basic description given by Frank Cooper.

I jotted a few notes on one of my three-by-five cards. When I looked up, Marvin Busby stood in the open door. "Boudreaux?" Before I could nod, he added, "I'm Busby. Raiford said you wanted to talk to me about Carl Edwards." He ignored my black eye.

One thing was obvious. If Cooper's description of the man behind the mask was accurate, Marvin Busby could in no way fit that portrayal.

I remembered Judith Perry's slurred remark that Marvin Busby was a louse. I hadn't known what to expect, but when Busby entered, I tended to agree with her.

His complexion had a greasy sheen, and his black hair was slicked straight back, hanging almost to his unbuttoned collar, under which lay a loosened tie.

While he was not morbidly obese, Busby looked about forty or fifty pounds overweight. The pleats in his brown slacks were pleats in name only, for they were pulled tight across his abdomen, and his wrinkled shirt was working out from around his waist.

I gestured to the chair across the desk. "Sorry to take

you away from your work, but this will only take a few minutes."

He shrugged. "No problem. The work isn't going away." He laughed.

"Yeah, I know."

I expected him to respond as the others when I asked if he had any idea where Carl Edwards might have vanished.

"Find the nearest country with no extradition agreement with the U.S.," he replied, a smirk on his puffy face.

"Oh? Such as?"

"Beats me, but if I'd pulled off what he did, that's where I would go."

He seemed awfully sure of himself. "Did he say that?"

Busby laughed. "He didn't have to. If I'd lost everything I'd invested, I'd take that half million and find me a snug little place somewhere down in South America."

I shook my head. "I don't follow. What do you mean, lost everything?"

A crooked grin played over his face. "Carl Edwards invested in a gold mining scheme in Ghana and the whole thing blew up in his face when a coup overthrew the government and took over."

All I could do was stare at him in stunned disbelief.

I had just been handed one heck of a motive.

Collecting my thoughts, I asked, "So, you really believe Edwards was the brains behind the job, huh?"

He pursed his thick lips and nodded. "Who else?"

Even though I knew it was probably a mistake on my part, his smug attitude irritated me, and I couldn't resist the opening. "You," I said simply.

Chapter Thirteen

My words knocked the breath out of him. His eyes grew wide, and his jaw hit the floor. He sputtered, "W-What—?"

With a faint smile, I explained. "No offense intended, Mr. Busby. I know you weren't involved, but you do owe various shady characters a great deal of money. Isn't that right?"

He glared at me, his face frozen in suppressed fury. "That's a lie."

I leaned back and arched an eyebrow. "Does the name Trimunti mean anything to you? Frank Trimunti?"

The question shattered the rage on his face.

Remembering Chief Pachuca's warning, I continued, "I'm not suggesting you had anything to do with it. All I'm saying is that I know you owe Trimunti eight thousand, and in the last few months, you've lost over seventy grand."

A sheen of sweat covered his face. He licked at his fat lips. In a growl, he demanded, "So what? That's nobody's business."

I held up both hands to my shoulders, palms out. "Hey, I know. Nobody's saying it is. My only point is that Carl Edwards is not the only one who had motive for the job." I paused, and then added, "Do I think you had anything to do with it? No. All I really wanted to ask you was if in any of your conversations with Edwards, he'd ever mentioned someplace he would like to visit. That's all. And you told me."

He relaxed. After a few seconds, he grinned. "You had me going there."

"Sorry. I didn't mean to." It was a lie, but I told it with a straight face, and he believed me.

"As far as where he might be, I have no idea. We weren't close. Oh, we'd worked together for years, but he was a vice president, and I was one of the peons. We didn't run in the same circle. Of course, if I was out somewhere and spotted Carl, we'd wave. But that wasn't too often."

I wanted to make the sarcastic comment that the reason it wasn't too often was that Edwards didn't frequent illegal gambling salons, but I kept my mouth closed.

After Busby left, I jotted details on my note cards as well as a reminder to pursue the two leads I'd just been given; one being that Edwards had lost a bundle on gold investments, and the second to see just what important job Edwards had at work on February 3 that kept him from going home.

According to Raiford Lindsey, Edwards' wife and daughter had packed up his remaining personal items after the criminalists had taken what they wanted.

I glanced at my watch as I headed for my pickup. Almost 4:00. I couldn't help worrying about my old man, but I wanted to take a look at Edwards' desk calendar or desk pad. If he were like most organized businessmen, he maintained a daily log of things to do, routinely checking them off after they were accomplished. I was anxious to see what he had written for February 3.

* * *

During the drive to the police station, I pushed Edwards from my mind and concentrated on my old man's predicament.

Salinas Sal had been murdered by two hitmen, Hymie Weinshank being one of the killers. The other was either Maury Erickson or Alex White. The motive for Sal's death had to be his witnessing the transfer of a body from one car to the other at Barton Springs four or five weeks earlier.

According to Danny's snitches, Weinshank hung out at the Zuider Zee Bar and Grill on the river.

I flexed my fingers on the steering wheel and chewed on my bottom lip. A sense of guilt nagged at me as it had all afternoon. I drew a deep breath and released a long sigh. I knew the only way to assuage that guilty feeling was to give Pachuca Butcherman's version of the story. Besides, if it blew up in my face, if the chief learned I knew of it and had said nothing, I'd never get any help from him again.

That decided, I mentally made my to-do list. After checking with Chief Pachuca about looking at Edwards' belongings, I'd stop by the apartment with a bag of hamburgers and another case of beer for my old man. Then I'd head for the Edwards' in Brentwood Estates, and finish off the night by dropping in at the Zuider Zee and getting a look at Weinshank and his cohorts—if they showed.

Pachuca rolled his eyes when I opened the door. "Now what?" His gaze focused on my black eye.

I plastered a little-boy-lost grin on my face and replied, "I've got some information for you, and I need—I mean, I'd appreciate a favor."

He eyed me suspiciously, and then jabbed a meaty finger at the chair across his desk. "So?"

I plopped down in the chair and leaned forward. "A transient was beaten to death out at the rail yard a few nights back. Salinas Sal was the name he went by." Pachuca frowned, and I continued, "There's nothing high profile about it. I imagine a dozen a year turn up out there."

He grunted. "At least."

I explained how I became involved, that my old man was found passed out near Sal, and he was a suspect. "I have him out on bail. One of my sources on Sixth Street told me another transient who went by the name Butcherman had witnessed the murder." I paused, figuring that my next revelation would infuriate Chief Pachuca.

"Now, Chief, I know you're stretched thin, and the truth, with transients passing through—" I hesitated, uncertain just how to say they were usually given little concern. "Well, sometimes poor slobs like Sal kind of fall through the cracks."

He studied me a moment, and then nodded. "Go on."

"Anyway, I ran Butcherman down and asked him about it." Pachuca's face darkened. I continued hastily, "Two nights earlier, he saw two men beat Sal. My old man was passed out nearby. The two spotted Butcherman, but he ditched them." I paused. "A couple nights back we were in Wichie's Last Chance Bar down on Sixth Street when two goons burst in and chased Butcherman out the back door." I laid my finger on the knot over my left eye. "That's where this and the black eye came from."

He curled one side of his lips. "It improves your looks."

"You bet. Anyway, one of the goon's face was scarred with acne. A source I'd rather not mention said that it sounded like a guy named Hymie Weinshank. There was a second dude, but I didn't get a chance to see him. Hymie runs with Maury Erickson and Alex White."

Pachuca leaned forward. "Don't keep nothing from me, Boudreaux. Who told you about Hymie?"

I lifted my eyebrows. "O'Banion."

The chief studied me a moment, and then nodded. "He ought to know. Is that all?"

"No. The story gets a little more intriguing. According to Butcherman, Sal told him that early in February, he was sleeping under a picnic table at Barton Springs, and he woke up to see two men hauling a body out of one car and dumping it in the trunk of another. They spotted Sal. He managed to get away, but he heard one of them say he'd recognized Sal."

Pachuca eyed me skeptically. "So why didn't he get out of town?"

"He did. San Antone. He was heading to Fort Worth when the train made a layover here. He made the mistake of going down Sixth Street to pick up a few bucks."

"Not too smart."

Thinking of my old man, I replied, "Nope. None of those old boys are what you'd call rocket scientists. Anyway, I wanted you to know in case there were any reports of missing persons around early February."

Without replying, he turned to his computer and drew up a file. After studying it a few moments, he glanced over his shoulder. "About half a dozen missing, and your Carl Edwards is one of them."

I nodded, having made no previous connection, but now a crazy idea popped into my head.

"Now," he growled, breaking into my thoughts. "What's the favor?"

"Huh? Oh, I was wondering if you'd had any luck on the information the psychic gave us."

"Not yet. Is that the favor?"

"No, not really. I'd like to look over the evidence from Edwards' desk."

"Why?"

"There's a possibility he jotted down a destination. Something. I don't know what." I grinned sheepishly. "I know it's a crazy hunch, but hey, who knows?"

He studied me a moment. "Tell you what. Tell Bob Ray to let you sign for whatever evidence you want. No sense in you sitting down there all night."

"Thanks, Chief. You're a gentleman and a scholar."

He waved me out of his office. "And you're full of it. Now get out of here."

Chapter Fourteen

I pulled up to my apartment thirty minutes later with a case of Old Milwaukee and a bag of burgers and fries.

I wrinkled my nose when I opened the apartment door. My old man still hadn't bathed, but at least he had donned his old clothes that I had run through the washer twice, each time with a copious amount of bleach. I couldn't complain. Part of him was clean. He was slumped on the couch in front of the TV, a cigarette in one hand and a beer in the other. At least, I told myself, he had not run off somewhere. I held up the bag of burgers. "Here's dinner," I announced, setting the bag on the snack bar and sliding the case of beer in the refrigerator.

I had considered leaving the box of evidence at my apartment, but I didn't trust him. It would be safer locked in my toolbox in the bed of my pickup.

"Well, boy. What did you find out today?"

"Getting closer," I replied, not wanting to go into any detail. "I've got an appointment tonight that might shed more light on the situation."

He shrugged, returning to the couch with a burger in one hand, a beer in the other, and a cigarette dangling from his cracked lips. I studied the contrary old man. The only reason he had consented to slip into his freshly washed clothes

91

is because I had warned him I planned to wash the sweat suit he had been wearing even if he was still in it.

An impish grin played over my lips as I paused in the bedroom doorway. I had an idea how to get him to clean up. "Like I said, I've got a couple of appointments tonight. If things turn out the way I think, you might go before the judge in the morning. Get in there and shower and shave tonight. I'll bring you some new clothes back."

He turned to me, his black eyes filled with anticipation. "That mean I can get out of this town?"

With a shrug, I replied, "We'll see tomorrow if the judge gets around to you. Just be ready."

I didn't know if my ruse would work or not, but it was a shot. I'm not particularly fastidious, but after a few days of the overpowering stench of dried sweat and a dirt-caked body, I had to have some relief.

Before I left that night, I switched license plates, a move I usually pull when I'm venturing into an environment where I want to evade identification. A local curio and joke shop down on Sixth Street made personalized license plates to decorate bedrooms and dens or whatever. I had one made that read TOOBAD, and on occasions such as tonight, I popped it on, and then clamped the legitimate plate in front of it. Removal of the legit plate took mere seconds.

I pulled into a Walmart on the way to the Edwards' and picked up a couple of shirts, a change of underwear, and two pair of jeans for John Roney. During the drive to the Edwards', I decided not to mention Busby's specific assertion that Edwards had lost everything in his gold investment.

* * *

Streetlights lit the well-maintained streets of Brentwood Estates. I pulled into the Edwards' driveway, and Debbie met me at the door.

Her smile couldn't hide the worry on her face. She led the way into the den, where Mrs. Edwards rose and greeted me. I could see the anxiety in her face also. "I hope you have some good news for us, Tony," she said softly. "We're worried sick."

I shook my head. "I wish I did too. I talked to the police an hour ago. Nothing has turned up, but then they've only been looking for a day."

Debbie sat on the couch and dropped her head to her chest. She looked up at me, her eyes welling with tears. "It's just that I feel so helpless."

I sat beside her and put my arm about her shoulders. I'd forgotten just how small she was. "We all feel like that, but we shouldn't. We—you and your mother—we're doing all we can."

Mrs. Edwards gasped. "Dear me, I forgot my manners. Would you care for some coffee, Tony?"

I declined. "No, thanks, but I've got a couple of questions you might be able to answer."

She sat on the edge of the overstuffed chair at the end of the coffee table, hands folded demurely in her lap. "Certainly."

"First, did your husband ever mention a place called Lost Lake? It's a fishing village in New Mexico."

She and Debbie frowned at each other, and she shook her head. "No. Is it important?"

With a sheepish grin, I replied, "I don't know yet. Now, your husband's investments. Are you familiar with them?"

She gave me an embarrassed smile. "I'm afraid not. Carl

handled all the money. But you might ask his CPA, Dillon Packard of Packard and Packard Accounting. Carl and Dill have worked together for years. He knows everything there is to know about our financial situation."

I frowned. "All right, but tell me, with Mr. Edwards gone, who takes care of the bills?"

Debbie spoke up. "Dill. Pop and Mom use credit cards on everything. The bills go to the accountants, and they take care of them. Pop gets—" She hesitated with a grimace. "Pop got a monthly statement from them. You want their number?"

"No. They're in the directory, right?"

"Yes."

"Just do me a favor and call Packard in the morning first thing. Tell him I'm going to drop by."

"By all means," replied Mrs. Edwards. "Is there anything else we can do?"

"One more thing. I'd like to look through your husband's personal effects that you brought home from his office."

She and Debbie exchanged puzzled looks, but she smiled and replied, "Certainly, but what for?"

"On February 3, when your husband went to work, he had a bad cold. You remember that?"

Debbie looked at her mother expectantly. Her mother nodded. "Yes. Now that you remind me. Carl could barely talk."

"That's what I learned. One of his co-workers suggested he go home, but he told them he couldn't. He had a job he had to take care of. Now, I'm hoping somewhere in his effects is a hint of that job."

Debbie's face blanched. "February 3? That's the day the armored car was robbed." Her eyes grew wide in alarm, and she turned to her mother, her fists pressed against her lips. "Mother! You don't think—"

"Of course not," Mrs. Edwards shot back. "Your father is the most honest and decent man in this world. You should be ashamed of yourself for even thinking such a horrible thought." She pushed to her feet. "The items are in the den, Tony. This way."

I tagged after her, but my feelings were leaning in the same direction as Debbie's. Edwards' remark could mean anything, but presently it appeared to be another brick in the ever-growing foundation for the wall of guilt building up around him.

Stacked beside the desk were three boxes of odds and ends, knickknacks, family pictures, and a pile of civic awards from public service clubs such as Kiwanis, Rotary, various churches, schools, and a dozen other organizations.

But nothing to suggest the importance of February 3.

Before I left, Debbie showed me a map spread on her father's desk. It was one of Austin and the surrounding countryside. From the credit union, she had drawn a series of pie-shaped wedges radiating to the county line.

"I know it might look silly to a professional like you, Tony, but we're out searching also. See this section right here." She touched a manicured nail to a wedge that had been yellowed in. "That's where we searched today. We drove all over, and every time we came to a gully or canyon or anything like that, we searched it."

I placed my hand on hers. "I think that's a magnificent idea." And it was. The search kept them busy, which was much better than sitting home and moping.

She smiled up at me, and I felt her fingers entwine mine. Her face grew serious. "Where did we go wrong, Tony?"

I stared at her. How do you tell someone the feeling is not there, was never there? I couldn't, so I did what I usually do in an awkward situation, I joked. "We didn't go wrong. You got lucky, Debbie, and got rid of me. I'm bad news. Always have been, and always will be." I laughed and pulled away.

She forced a laugh. "Maybe so." But there was no conviction in her voice.

As I headed for Lake Austin Boulevard along the banks of the Colorado River, I couldn't get Debbie's question out of my mind.

We'd both started teaching English the same year at Madison High School, a school where administrators weren't too concerned with what was taught as long as the parents were kept happy. The core curriculum of the school was not English or math or science, but football, the report card for every community in the great state of Texas.

Debbie was all any man could wish for, gracious, understanding, and compassionate. We had fun together, but being with her was like being with one of the boys.

After she and I drifted apart, I dated a little here and a little there. My experience with my first marriage had provided enough trauma to last me until the chickens came home to roost.

I shook my head in frustration. While a professional distance is essential in a PI/client relationship, I knew it would be hard with Debbie. And I had no idea how I was going to handle it.

Sandwiched between Bernie's Crab Shack and Travis County Canoe Trips, the Zuider Zee Bar and Grill perched on the river side of Lake Austin Boulevard, looking down on the black waters of the Colorado River a hundred feet below. The 1950s building was outlined with green neon, the same color as the flashing Zuider Zee sign above the canopied entrance.

I drove past and pulled onto the shoulder. Climbing out, I walked around the pickup, kicking the tires and checking oncoming traffic. I paused by the tailgate, and when I spotted a break in traffic, I quickly removed the license plate, leaving the fake one.

Moments later, I pulled into the parking lot, which was sparsely filled with two or three medium-sized vehicles that were probably Hondas or Toyotas, and a few larger cars of American manufacture. Don't ask me what makes. They all look the same to me. The only one I recognized was the angular lines of a Cadillac, and that was because my pal Jack Edney had just purchased a new Cadillac convertible at the insistence of his wife, Diane, my ex.

Even though Diane ended up with all we had except Oscar, an albino tiger barb fish with brain damage, our divorce for the most part was amicable. She was Jack's handful now.

Inside, the décor smacked of the fifties. A dozen or so customers sat in booths and at the bar. I slid onto a stool upholstered in black plastic, and I couldn't help noticing that the seat next to me had a slash in it from which some sort of gray padding bulged.

I knew right then the décor was not architecturally retro to the fifties, but from the actual fifties itself. Indirect lighting from valances at the top of the walls was the only illumination except for the red, green, and yellow strobe flashes from the jukebox. At the far end of the room, planter boxes containing broad-leafed exotic plants of plastic sat on two half walls in front of the restrooms.

The bartender came up to me. "What'll it be, pal." His eyes drifted to the knot on my forehead.

"Draft beer. Miller Lite if you got it."

"Coming right up."

I studied him as he drew the Miller. Average looking, about fifty. He parted his thinning hair in the middle. I couldn't quite put my finger on it, but there was something about his face that made me believe those fifty-plus years had been pretty rugged, like he'd been stomped on, tossed about, and finally kicked out.

To my left, a few stools away, sat a couple. He wore a suit, and his hair was slicked back. Wearing a low-cut floral dress, she sat staring blankly at him, one leg crossed over the other, a cigarette dangling from between her fingers.

The bartender slid the beer in front of me, and I laid down a fiver. I would allow myself this one. While he made change, I peered into the mirror over the highboy behind the bar.

Only two of the dozen or so booths around the wall were occupied, both by couples.

Hymie Weinshank was not here. I wasn't surprised. I'd figured I might have to hang out several nights before I spotted him. I just hoped no one who knew me showed up. Seems like I always run into an acquaintance when I'm somewhere or with someone I shouldn't be. That's why I've never gone to Hooter's.

The bartender slid my change on the bar. "Thanks," I said, leaving the change where it was.

He studied me a few moments while he dried a couple of beer mugs. "Ain't seen you around."

My hand wrapped around the draft. There was ice around the rim. "Just got in. Insurance. Might be around a few days."

Nodding slowly, he cut his eyes in one direction and then

the other. In a conspiratorial tone, he whispered, "You looking for any action?" He gestured with curled fingers as if he were rolling craps.

With a laugh, I shook my head. "Nope. Married. The little lady would kill me if I lost any money." I hooked my thumb over my shoulder. "I started to get a bite next door at the Crab Shack, but decided to wet my whistle first."

He grinned. "Glad to have you. Need anything, give me a yell. Name's Harlon." He pointed to a door to the left of the restrooms. "We have a balcony out there overlooking the river. Kinda nice on a night like this with the stars out. Might have to watch out if you're allergic to cats. We got a bunch hanging around here."

I laughed. "Well, if I had my wife here, I'd take you up on it."

At that moment, the man to my left signaled the bartender.

I glanced at the clock above the highboy. 10:30. I figured I'd hang around until midnight, and then cut out.

I didn't have to wait. At that moment, the door swung open and a man with an acne-scarred face came inside.

Hymie Weinshank!

Chapter Fifteen

A taller man tagged behind Hymie.

Hymie was wearing the black leather jacket I had seen on him at Wichie's. The man with him wore a Houston Texans Windbreaker, a red one. He had a hatchet face and a hooked nose.

As Hymie passed the bar, the bartender nodded. "Hey, Hymie, Alex. How's it going?"

The two grunted and continued to the rear where they disappeared through a door on the right side of the restrooms.

I glanced at the door through which they had disappeared. I stretched my arms over my head and pushed the mug away. Leaving the change from the fiver on the bar, I slid off the stool. "Thanks, Harlon."

He lifted an eyebrow. "That was a short visit. You didn't drink your beer."

Patting my stomach, I laughed. "I'm starving. Hey, can I leave my pickup out front while I step next door?"

"Sure. We ain't that busy tonight." He slid the change into his hand and wiped the bar with a towel. "No problem at all."

Privet hedges separated the two businesses. I circled the hedge, peering at the rear of the Zuider Zee. The glow of its green neon lights eerily illumined the front and a portion of the side of the building. In the darkness beyond the glow, light shone from a window, and as close as I could figure, that was the room into which Hymie and Alex had disappeared.

I slipped into the darkness.

The building sat on a massive concrete slab cantilevered over the sloping bluff and supported by oversize concrete piers sunk in the limestone rock.

Walks with rails ran along the side of the building to the balcony. I grimaced. If I got caught out at the end of the balcony, there was nowhere to go except down. It was a hundred foot drop to the river, and I had never been any good at high diving.

Still, my curiosity nagged at me to peek in the window.

The glow of the neon lit the first few feet of the walk, so I stayed behind the hedge until I was beyond the neon glow. The sidewalk was a couple of feet above my head. Somehow, I managed to haul my aging body up and over the railing.

I crouched in the darkness, looking one way and then another with sweat pouring off my face and my breath coming in ragged gasps. A dim green light glowed from the balcony at the far end of the walk. As long as I remained in the dark, I was safe.

Easing down the walk, I crouched beneath the window. Venetian blinds covered it, but one of the slats had hung up on the lines, leaving a tiny gap though which I could peer. The window was opened slightly at the bottom, allowing muted voices to squeeze out. I looked both ways again. Laughter came from the balcony around the corner. I hoped no one decided to take a stroll.

Easing forward, I squinted through the gap. Hymie and

Alex were facing a man sitting in a leather office chair with its back to me. All I could see were his arms on the armrests. He wore a tan jacket and a gold wedding ring on his left hand.

Hymie wore an angry frown. "Why not now?"

A voice came from the chair. "Too soon."

Suddenly, I heard a cat meow. I glanced down and in the shadows cast by the glowing neon, I made out a full-grown calico. She curled around my ankles and purred like the proverbial motorboat. I quickly picked her up and pressed her to my chest, gently rubbing between her ears and whispering to calm her purring. "Nice girl, nice girl. Just—"

At that moment, a woman's strident voice behind me shouted, "What are you doing here, you pervert?" I spun to see a woman in a chic dress with a drink in her hand staring at me. "What—"

Before she uttered another word, I tossed her the calico and raced down the walk. Behind me came the startled yowling and hissing of an enraged cat followed by the horrified screams of a terrified woman.

Before I reached the green neon glow, I climbed over the rail and disappeared into the darkness beneath the slab on which the Zuider Zee was built.

I glanced at the restaurant next door. Just as I started to dash for it, a shadow appeared on the limestone slope between me and the crab shack.

From above, I heard a voice. It was Hymie's. "Check under the building, Alex. I'll look up here. Something's fishy. The dame said she saw somebody at the window."

I darted beneath the Zuider Zee. A dozen huge concrete beams ran the length of the slab on which it sat. Steel rods ran between the beams offering storage for canoes, outdoor furniture, and a dozen various assortments of items.

I managed to swing up above the rods into the darkness,

rolled over, and waited. Facing down, my chest and arms rested on one rod and my knees on another. I had a snug little hidey-hole that I wasn't about to give up.

A few minutes later, a shadow stumbled across the limestone slope and into the darkness cast by the slab.

Hymie called out from above, "Find anyone?"

The shadow, which was no more than five feet from me, replied, "I can't see nothing down here, Hymie."

"Snap on your lighter, dummy."

"Yeah. I didn't think about that."

I couldn't stay put. When his lighter flared, he'd be staring straight into my face. Taking a deep breath, I eased back, gripped a rod firmly, and then swung down, pulling my legs up so I could strike Alex in the chest.

He grunted when my feet slammed into him.

With a wild scream, he hit the rocky slope and tumbled head over heels toward the river. Suddenly, there was a silence, and moments later a splash.

Overhead, I heard Hymie cursing.

Staying in the shadows, I slipped through the hedge and, my pulse racing, darted into Bernie's Crab Shack.

Despite the hour, they were busy.

I spotted a vacant table. I hurried to it, picking up a glass of tea from the waitstaff's serving table.

Moments later, a young woman wearing a knee-length apron with crabs embroidered on it sidled up to my table to take my order.

"Crabs and fried shrimp," I replied.

She nodded and pointed her pencil to the salad bar. "Help yourself."

Bernie's was fast. Before I got back to my table with my salad, a platter of soft-shell crabs, fried shrimp, French fries, and rolls were waiting for me.

I wasn't hungry, but I picked at the platter before me.

A motion from the corner of my eye caught my attention. I glanced up, and then quickly looked away.

Standing in the door was Harlon, the bartender, and Hymie.

I drew a deep breath and took another bite of crab. I could feel their eyes on me.

After they left, my imagination ran wild. Now what? Would they wait until I left and snatch me? Work me over like they had Sal? Or simply shoot me and dump me somewhere?

My nerves were ready to snap as I left Bernie's and headed for my pickup in the Zuider Zee parking lot. To my surprise and relief, the lot was empty. I climbed into my Silverado and drove away without incident.

The roads were still busy. I glanced in the rearview mirror and saw a dozen lights behind me. Over the next few miles, I turned several times, carefully watching the lights in the mirror, and then I headed for Zilker Park on the Colorado.

After wandering the almost deserted lanes for thirty minutes, I took Barton Springs Road over to Congress Avenue and then headed on home.

I couldn't help wondering about the identity of the guy talking to Hymie and Alex.

When I parked in the drive, I switched license plates again. I grimaced when I spotted the box of evidence Pachuca had permitted me to take. I'd go in early in the morning and peruse the information.

My old man was slouched on the couch watching soap opera reruns on TV with a cigarette in one hand and a beer in the other. "Out of burgers," he muttered, turning back to his program.

"No problem." To my delight, he had done as I'd asked, showered, shaved, and slipped into a clean sweat suit. Of course, he left his old rags where he'd dropped them, just as he did the three towels he used. But I was not about to complain. I'd much rather pick up after him than smell him.

I dropped the bags of new clothes on the coffee table. "Here you are."

He paid them no attention.

Although it was almost midnight, I plopped down in front of the computer and pulled up my e-mail. I grinned when I spotted the message from Eddie Dyson.

My grin turned to a frown when I read his message. Usually a couple of days was all he needed, but a few problems had arisen. He promised results the next day.

I lay in bed that night trying to make sense of the last few days. To just about everyone except his family, it was a foregone conclusion that Carl Edwards was behind the heist.

From what personal knowledge I had of him combined with the opinions of most of his co-workers, I found it difficult to believe he was responsible.

But a searing question remained. If he were not behind the heist, why did he disappear? Why did he miss the San Francisco flight? On the other hand, if he were trying to disappear, why would he use his own name when purchasing the ticket?

Frustrated, I rolled over and closed my eyes, but sleep evaded me. I couldn't get Carl Edwards out of my mind. Then I remembered a hint Al Grogan once gave me after I hit a dead end on an insurance scam. "Kick the envelope apart. Work out of the box. Turn your theory a hundred and eighty degrees, and then try to solve it."

The hint worked, not all the time, but often enough to be effective. I rolled on my back and stared at the darkness above me. "All right," I muttered. "If Edwards didn't pull the job, then why is he missing?"

He lost money on a flyer in gold in Ghana, I reminded myself. So he made a bad investment. Surely he wouldn't have put everything in it. That didn't fit the profile of the man.

If, and I wasn't sure just how big an "if" the "if" was, but if he had not lost all his money, why disappear? Regardless of how much life insurance he carried, no company would pay off without a body, at least for several years. And I assumed he was smart enough to know that.

I sat up in bed and turned on the night-light. Usually when I work at night, I go into the living room, but my old man was sleeping, a state I much preferred.

On a pad, I jotted down the question, *If Edwards didn't pull the job, who did?*

Marvin Busby? I discounted him because of Cooper's description. Same with Larry Athens and Raiford Lindsey. Rita Johnson was too tall, but only by three or four inches. The only ones who were of similar size to Carl Edwards were Mary Louise Smith and Elizabeth Romero.

Somehow, I couldn't see either Romero or Smith pulling off an armored car robbery.

I muttered in disgust, "Now, Tony, where does that leave you? Not one soul at the credit union fits Cooper's description except Carl Edwards."

Then an idea hit, one I had never considered, and with it

an outrageous conclusion. *What if Cooper deliberately lied about the description?*

But why would he do that, I asked myself.

The answer hit me between the eyes. *Maybe because he pulled the job himself.*

Chapter Sixteen

I leaned back and stared, unseeing, at my closet door. I'd never been comfortable with the idea that an intelligent man like Carl Edwards would pull such a high-profile job. Of course, I couldn't explain the intended flight to San Francisco only hours after the heist went down, even though he didn't take the flight. Now, I know many criminals are so dumb they never think about a getaway until they have to do it. Edwards wasn't like that. If he had purchased the ticket a week earlier to escape the police, he would not have used his own name.

For some reason, he didn't show up. Why?

I caught my breath as an unwanted answer hit me. If I took that theory another step forward, logic would suggest that whoever perpetrated the heist might have killed Edwards. What if the slight man had walked in on the robbery while it was in progress? I hesitated. He would have had to blunder in after the robbers had bound and blindfolded the guards. Otherwise they would have seen him. I jotted a note to talk to one of the guards, but first I had to get Pachuca's okay.

I went back to my notes.

They couldn't have shot him, for according to Cooper, only one shot was fired, the one that wounded Frank Cooper, but they could have tied and blindfolded him as they had the guards. I circled the word *guards*, telling myself that they could verify the fact that only one shot was fired.

To my surprise, my old man was up and dressed the next morning even though I climbed out of bed an hour early. He looked like a different man with his hair combed and wearing fresh jeans and a new shirt that still had the wrinkles from being folded. "We going to see the judge this morning?" He shook his head. "I'm sure ready to shake the dust of this town from my heels."

I flipped on the coffeemaker and headed for the bathroom, experiencing a touch of guilt for lying to him, but at least he was clean. "I'll call the D.A. when they open and then give you a ring. I've got to get in early to catch up on some work."

When he nodded, I saw a glitter of hope in his eyes, and I felt like a heel for lying to him.

After depositing the box of evidence the criminalists had gathered at Edwards' office on my desk at work, I put coffee on to perk, and rolled up my sleeves. I glanced at my watch: 7:30. Packard and Packard Accounting opened at 9:00 probably. I made a note to call Debbie around 8:00 to remind her to give Dillon Packard a call.

Sometimes luck is like a crashing river racing down a canyon, and sometimes it's like a Louisiana bayou, moving slow and smooth. I had the good fortune to find that crashing river for thirty minutes after I opened the box of evidence, as I stumbled across what I was searching for.

On Edwards' desk pad on February 3 was the notation *Cummings, S.F.* I grinned and leaned back. Then a frown erased my smile. At first, I thought that I had found some support for my wild little theory that perhaps Edwards had not pulled the job. On the other hand, this Cummings joker could be Edwards' link to anything, even to the laundering of half a million bucks.

Just after I reminded Debbie to call Packard, Marty sauntered in, an hour earlier than he usually made it. From his unkempt dress, I guessed he'd never made it home the night before, although unkempt seemed to be the style he favored. He stopped at my desk.

"How's the Edwards thing going?"

I shook my head. "Slow. If he was planning on disappearing, he kept mighty quiet about it. The only leads I have are a flight to San Francisco he didn't take, and the mention of a resort in New Mexico where he went to fish."

He shrugged. "Check them out."

I slid the folders containing the evidence back in the box. "I plan on it."

I don't know what I expected of Packard and Packard Accounting, perhaps a sordid little room with half a dozen sallow-faced men hunched over wooden desks with pencils in their hands, a la Charles Dickens' *Christmas Carol.*

Instead, it was an airy office with expansive glass walls containing a dozen employees behind computers. I stopped at the receptionist's desk and identified myself. "I believe Dillon Packard is expecting me."

Smiling brightly, she spoke into a telephone, and then indicated a hall at the rear of the office. "Third door on the left."

The name Dillon Packard suggested vitality and strength. I was surprised to see a slender man about seventy with a white tonsure about his head that was part of the neatly trimmed white beard and sideburns.

He surprised me again when he swiftly strode across the floor and seized my hand in a firm grip. His eyes twinkled. "Mr. Boudreaux. I'm happy to meet you. Debbie Edwards said you were coming." He indicated a chair in front of a massive desk that sported a Spanish granite top. "Please."

I sat, and he slid into a plush leather chair behind the desk and leaned back. I couldn't help noticing how perfectly his suit coat draped from his shoulders. I glanced sheepishly at my tweed jacket with the worn leather patches on the elbows.

He smiled. "Now, what can I do for you? All Debbie said was that you wanted to talk to me about her father."

"That's right. You see, Mrs. Edwards and Debbie hired me to find their father. He's been missing several weeks."

The smile faded from his face. "I know."

"In trying to find him, I ran into a couple of curious incidents that you, as his accountant, probably have knowledge of."

"Certainly, certainly." He nodded emphatically, a thin smile on his face.

"I was told he lost a large sum of money in a gold investment in Ghana."

Dillon studied me a moment, his smile fading. "I'm sorry, but that's private information, Mr. Boudreaux."

His conscientious circumspection both impressed and irritated me. "Look. I'm working for Debbie and her mother. If you want, I'll haul them in here and have them ask the question."

He considered my reply. Finally, he dipped his head. "That is correct."

"How much?"

The older man hesitated again. I gave him a silly grin as if to say, *Okay, I'll go get Debbie and her mother.* With a hint of resignation, he replied, "Seven hundred and thirty thousand dollars."

I whistled to myself. "Will such a loss force him into bankruptcy?"

Once again, he struggled with his sense of ethics before answering. "I hope you understand my reticence in revealing Mr. Edwards' financial status to you, Mr. Boudreaux. I've worked with Carl for over forty years. It's difficult to reveal such private information."

I fixed my eyes on his. "If this information will help us find him, don't you think it's worth it?"

He tried to look behind the determination in my eyes. "Do you think he's dead?"

With a shrug, I replied, "I don't know. That's what his family wants to know. If you can help them find some closure, one way or another, they'll forever be grateful."

Finally, he shook his head. "Far from bankruptcy, Mr. Boudreaux. Carl was a prudent investor." With a wave of his hand, he added, "No specific figures, but he has more than twice that in assets."

A smug feeling of satisfaction came over me. Those last words convinced me that Carl Edwards had no part in the robbery. "He booked a flight to San Francisco on February 3 to see someone named Cummings. Any idea?"

His face grew animated. "Oh, yes. J.J. Cummings was the leading investor in the gold mining venture in Ghana. He and Carl had a scheduled meeting with the leaders of the Ghana coup. J.J. felt they could work a deal by cutting the coup in on the profits." He paused. "He kept calling about Carl, wanting to know where he was. Finally, he had to make the decisions himself."

"And?"

With a wry grin, he replied, "The rebels decided they'd take all the profits."

"Generous of them, huh?" I paused a moment. "Let me ask a personal question if you don't mind, Mr. Packard."

A terse smile tightened his lips. "Certainly."

"Edwards has been gone over a month. Have you contacted his wife about his affairs?"

The slender man stiffened. I would have sworn his bald pate turned red. With a hint of disdain, he replied, "Certainly. On three different occasions I contacted Mrs. Edwards and asked if I could visit with her to inform her of the status of her finances. She refused."

When I arched an eyebrow, he continued, "She insisted on waiting until he returned." He drew a deep breath. "What was I to do?"

"Not much," I replied, rising and offering my hand. "Thanks for your help."

A few moments later, I slid into my pickup and sat staring at the expansive glass building. I couldn't decide if I should apprise Chief Pachuca of my theory, or continue digging.

"Don't be an idiot, Tony," I muttered. "Pachuca finds out you're investigating the robbery, you're dead meat."

I started the pickup and headed for the police station, ostensibly to drop off the box of evidence and ask the chief's permission to talk to the security guards who had staffed the armored car the day of the robbery.

After dropping the box off to Bob Ray Burrus in the Evidence Room, I went upstairs and thanked the chief once again.

"Find anything helpful?"

"Not much. You know that flight he missed to San Francisco?"

Pachuca shrugged. "What about it?"

"It was to see about an investment that went bad."

He grunted. "Bad investments, huh? No wonder he pulled the job."

I just shrugged and asked if I could question the armored car guards to see if they'd overhead anything.

"I don't see why not." He reached for the phone. "How soon can you get over there?"

"Anytime," I replied, surprised at his willingness to help. "Anytime."

A few moments later, he replaced the receiver and looked up at me. "Get over to Quad-County Armored Car Services and ask for Matt Bellows. He'll put you in touch with the guards."

Chapter Seventeen

Matt Bellows was a bear of a man, standing almost six-eight. I took in his neat uniform. The pleats were sharp and crisp, and there was no question in my mind that his uniforms were tailor-made. No way clothes off the rack would fit this behemoth. In fact, the only Gargantua around larger than Bellows was Danny O'Banion's bodyguard, Huey, who, I mentioned earlier, could serve as a body double for Godzilla.

Bellows indicated a chair in front of his desk and flipped a switch on the office intercom. "Send Ramsey and Borke in."

Moments later, two uniformed security guards entered, nodded to Bellows, and then looked curiously at me. Bellows introduced me. "He wants to ask about the robbery at Tri-District."

The two looked at each other, and then shrugged. "Shoot," replied the smaller of the two.

"Tell me about the robbery."

"From the beginning?"

"Yes."

He glanced at Bellows, who nodded once again. "Go ahead, Jack."

"Not much to tell. There was a green light above the side door. That was their way of telling us to come on in. We figured the teller in the anteroom next to the vault saw us coming and opened it. Eddie and me here carried the bags in. Two goons in gorilla masks held guns on us. They made us undress, and then tied and blindfolded us. I heard some noise—scuffling like, you know? I learned later they put on our uniforms, and Carmen, our guard in the back of the truck, thought it was us. They tied and blindfolded her." He glanced up at the one named Eddie. "That's about it, huh?"

"Yep."

"So you only saw two?"

"Yeah," replied the first one.

"Could you describe them?"

Eddie chuckled. "They was wearing masks, remember?"

"Yeah, but I mean size. Tall, skinny, fat, whatever."

Jack shrugged. "About average. Like me and Eddie here."

I nodded. "Go on."

"Not much more," Eddie said. "Oh, yeah, before they went out to the truck, someone else came in. We could hear them whispering. Then one or two left."

"Did you hear anything that might suggest where they were headed after leaving?"

Eddie pursed his lips. "Nah. Then we heard someone else come in." He hesitated. "Jack and me here have talked about it. Someone came in and said something like 'what' or something. Then there was a thud and someone fell to the floor. For a couple of minutes you could hear them coming and going, and then there was a gunshot, and the door slammed shut."

Jack shook his head. "Scared the bejeebies out of me. I thought they was going to kill us right there."

"Yeah." Eddie shook his head. "I was sure praying hard."

I leaned forward. "You said that whoever came in the second time said something. Can you remember what it was?"

Jack spoke up. "Nothing really. It was kind of a surprised sort of expression, you know, like 'what' or something like that."

"One thing I remember about the voice, though, is that it sounded kind of raspy."

I narrowed my eyes and held my breath. "Like laryngitis, maybe?"

The two guards looked at each other and nodded simultaneously. "Yeah, like laryngitis," replied Eddie.

I cleared my throat. "Let me get this straight. You said someone came in and said something like 'what.' Then there was a thud and someone fell to the floor."

"Yeah. He groaned before he fell to the floor, and then we heard them leave and come back for a minute or so."

"And then the gunshot?"

"Yeah."

Bellows spoke up. "Whoever them dudes was, they wiped the truck clean when they left it in a deserted warehouse in downtown Austin." He paused. "They knew what they were doing."

I lifted an eyebrow. "Sounds like it." Extending my hand, I thanked them. As they turned to leave, it struck me the two guards were about the same height as Hymie and Alex.

An idea popped into my head. Was it possible? Could Carl Edwards have been the one who walked in on the heist and was knocked to the floor? I shook my head. Ludicrous. Impossible. But—

Heading back to the office, I swung by the D.A.'s, hoping to catch Mark Swain and get an update on my old man's paperwork. I was tempted to tell him what I had learned about Hymie Weinshank and Alex White, but decided against it. I had nothing substantial to prove they had murdered Salinas Sal or Butcherman.

Mark thumbed through the stack of papers on his desk. "Nope. Nothing here." He looked up at me. "It's only been a few days, hasn't it?"

"Yeah."

"Give it time. Get hold of me—" He glanced at his calendar pad. "Say next Wednesday. We ought to know something by then."

Usually, I do my best thinking at home, but with my old man there, I swung by the office, hoping for a little solitude so I could untangle the maze of theories bouncing around in my skull.

The only one in at the office was Doreen Patterson, the rookie on our staff. I'd help break Doreen in a few months earlier.

She smiled brightly when she spotted me. "Hey, stranger. Where you been keeping yourself?"

"Busy," I replied, sliding behind my computer. "You?"

She reached into a desk drawer and pulled out a digital camera the size of a deck of cards. "Same old, same old." She dropped the camera in her jacket pocket. "Sorry to rush, but I got a date with a cheating wife." She patted her pocket.

I grinned. "Good luck."

After the door closed behind her, leaving me in the office by myself, I pulled out my stack of three-by-five cards and booted up my computer. The last few days had been so hectic, I'd never really taken time to thoroughly analyze all I had learned.

That probably explained why I felt as if I were going in

circles. I had a great deal of information, but very few ideas on which to hang any of it. And from past experience, I knew that unless I took time to massage the information, to ruminate over it, the possibility of overlooking pertinent details was inevitable.

I created a folder on the Tri-District Credit Union, and the first file I began work on was Carl Edwards.

Including my personal knowledge of the man as well as the opinions of those with whom he worked, I was firmly convinced the slight man had not masterminded the heist, a conviction that could cause me more problems than a bayou full of alligators if Chief Ramon Pachuca ever discovered I was prying into police business.

The evidence against Edwards was devastating, especially the eyewitness testimony of Frank Cooper, who recognized Edwards' voice as well as the herringbone suit the slight man had been wearing.

In the seedy world of crime, perps usually have three factors driving them: motive, opportunity, and means.

Edwards had opportunity and means but, to me, no motive.

Sure, Marvin Busby had said Edwards had lost everything in the gold mining scheme in Ghana, but Edwards' CPA disputed the statement. Even after the almost three-quarters of a million the coup commandeered, his estate was still worth a million and a half.

I studied the screen thoughtfully. No way could I see motive here. I pushed back from my desk and headed for the coffee pot. I shivered after the first sip. Talk about clearing the sinuses. It was thick enough to slap on a piece of bread like peanut butter.

Standing behind my chair, I stared down at the screen. The next piece of incriminating evidence was the flight to San Francisco, the one Edwards never made.

To the police, that ticket was the final nail in Edwards' figurative coffin, but if the investigator had pursued the trail a tad farther, he would have discovered the true purpose of the trip, a perfectly legitimate explanation, to negotiate with the Ghana rebels. But, like much evidence, it was not thoroughly analyzed, which prompted an erroneous interpretation.

I sipped the coffee and once again shivered, this time because at that moment, I somehow knew Carl Edwards was dead. I couldn't prove it, but if he were the one who fell to the floor during the heist, he had to be. In fact, I told myself, taking another leap forward, Carl Edwards could have been the body Salinas Sal saw being transferred from one car to another that night at Barton Springs.

Chapter Eighteen

I started to create a file for Raiford Lindsey, the president of the credit union, before I realized I had yet to hear from Eddie Dyson on either Lindsey or Frank Cooper.

Going online, I e-mailed Eddie an inquiry, and then returned to my work.

I built a file for Cooper, based upon our conversation the day he walked with me to my pickup.

He identified Edwards by the herringbone suit and his voice. He said he had simply wandered into the anteroom next to the vault and stumbled onto the heist. Edwards then shot him. He also testified that the slight man wore gloves.

Leaning back, I reread the file, and then thumbed back through my cards in case I had left out any pertinent information. I noted where I had asked Cooper if Edwards had ever mentioned a fishing trip at Falcon Reservoir, and he'd said no. I spotted his remark that Edwards had ordered him to lie down. I stared at the ceiling trying to recall his words. I checked my cards. I would have sworn he said Edwards shouted at him to lie down. Obviously, I had failed to document that remark.

Still, the two guards had only said they heard voices. I made a note to check with them.

My next file was on Elizabeth Romero, Lindsey's executive secretary. Like ninety-nine percent of the employees, she could offer no motive for Edwards. She saw him that day, noting he could barely talk because of laryngitis from a cold that had him wheezing and hacking.

To finish off our conversation, she informed me that everyone in the credit union knew the armored car schedule.

My next file was Marla Jo Keeton, a perceptive employee who alleged Marvin Busby was in debt. She referred to one of the tellers, Judith Perry, as having a relationship with Busby. She also had informed me that even if she knew where Carl Edwards had gone, she would never tell.

At that moment, the phone rang. I answered it. Danny O'Banion's terse voice spoke. "Tony. We got your old man down here. You better come over."

Five of my apartments would fit in Danny's office. While neither he nor I could pronounce half the brands of his furniture and decorations, they were all expensive. So naturally, I cringed to see my old man sprawled on a white leather couch, his mouth gaping open and snoring like a chainsaw, and the mud from his heels smearing the cushions.

Before I could ask, Danny explained, "My boys picked him up at the Golden Gull Bar a couple of blocks from your place. Brought him down here and fed him some beer and hamburgers." A faint smile played over his boyish face. "He can't get in trouble here."

"Thanks."

Danny grew serious. "You know you can't trust him at your place all by his lonesome."

"Tell me something I don't know," I replied, a little testy.

Danny lifted an eyebrow. I shook my head. "Hey, I didn't mean nothing. I'm upset with him. I appreciate what you did."

He waved off my thank-you. "Forget it." He paused. "Tell you what. I know you're busy, and you can't keep an eye on him twenty-four/seven. Leave him here. I've got room."

I shook my head. "Thanks, but no thanks. That's too much trouble. I can take care of him."

Danny shrugged. "Whatever you say. The offer is always open."

Traffic was heavy when I left Danny's with John Roney leaning against the door, his head back on the seat, still snoring.

I-35 was bumper-to-bumper, side-by-side as far as the eye could see. One little fender bender, and the whole mess would be tied up for hours. That's why I usually opted for the business route. Lamar Street was choked also, but there were side streets that offered the opportunity to skirt any pileups.

Sometimes I'd laugh at the irony of modern progress. We built freeways to lessen traffic congestion only to have the interstate end up more congested than the streets they had been designed to alleviate traffic from. Crazy, huh?

My mind was a thousand miles away after leaving Danny's place. Without thinking, I hit the entry ramp for I-35 North before realizing what I had done. I cursed myself, then flexed my fingers about the wheel, and settled down to join the stampede of vehicles heading north.

Most of us were jammed too closely to worry about passing other cars, but there are always those who like to bob and weave, darting in front of one and then another. One of the problems interstates face is that, if you leave more than a few feet between you and the car ahead, some joker will consider it a double-dog-dare challenge to shoehorn a twenty-foot-long vehicle into a fifteen-foot opening.

I'm a coward when it comes to traffic. I always stay in the outside lane and within the speed limit. After some experience, you learn to ignore the shouts and gestures tossed at you.

When the massive Peterbilt rolled up on my left, I gave it a cursory glance, but then as we started to approach an overpass, it eased toward me.

I honked, but it kept coming. "Hey, buddy, back off," I shouted, knowing the driver couldn't hear me. I shot a glance at the overpass. Off to my right was a sloping grassy median stretching gently to the feeder road some hundred feet distant.

The Peterbilt moved closer.

I honked again.

The massive tractor came even closer.

My tires hit the small curb. I fought the wheel.

The overpass guardrails loomed larger. And just beyond the guardrails was a fifty-foot drop straight down to the highway below. If I hit the rails, I'd flip head over heels to the boulevard below.

I had a choice: the guardrails or the grass.

Taking a deep breath, I jerked the wheel to the right and shot down the grassy slope, at the same time slamming on my brakes and fighting for control of the pickup.

The feeder road, jammed with traffic, loomed ahead. Slamming on my emergency brake, I spun the wheel hard to the left, sending the pickup into a 180-degree spin, and coming to a sliding halt only inches from the feeder road.

I closed my eyes and breathed a sigh of relief, at the same time cursing the careless driver of the big rig.

I glanced at my old man, who was rubbing his bony fists into his eyes. He looked around and grumbled, "What's going on? Don't you know how to drive, boy?"

I just stared at him. Finally after my nerves settled, I pulled onto the feeder road and headed home. My old man had gone back to sleep, a state from which he did not emerge until we pulled into the drive. He awakened long enough to stagger inside and collapse on the couch.

I went into the bathroom and washed my face. I stared at myself in the mirror. My black eye was beginning to turn yellow, and the knot was slowly shrinking.

I slipped behind my computer and continued work on my files. I glanced at my note cards. Judith Perry was next. A slow grin played over my face when I remembered how infuriated she had become with Marvin Busby.

Before I could begin work on her file, an e-mail message beeped. Anxiously I went to my mailbox, hoping for a response from Eddie Dyson.

There was one, but not what I expected. The message was from my ISP's mail administrator stating that there was no record of such an address for Eddie Dyson.

I muttered a short curse. There was no logic in cyberspace, just a bunch of loonies buzzing around changing addresses at will. Chances were in ten minutes, I'd have a response from Eddie.

At that moment, the phone rang. It was Neon Larry. "Tony. What's up?"

"Nothing. What's the problem?"

His voice became guarded. "I ain't sure, but Goofyfoot came by a few minutes ago. He's got something I think you need to hear."

I drew a deep breath and closed my eyes. I had about all I could handle right now. "Can't it wait until tomorrow?"

Neon Larry grunted. "I ain't sure. I don't think so. From the way he talked, some goons is planning on doing something to your old man, maybe waste him."

Chapter Nineteen

I glanced over my shoulder at my old man, who was still snoozing on the couch. "What is this, Larry? Some kind of joke?"

"Nah. That's what Goofyfoot told me. I don't know," he added, half serious, half joking. "The old bum might have got some bad whiskey, but I figured you ought to know about it."

I paused a moment to consider my next step. "If you see Goofyfoot around, tell him to wait. I'll be down in about an hour. Feed him beer to keep him there. I'll pay you."

Without replacing the receiver, I broke the connection, and then dialed Jack Edney, an old friend and nouveau millionaire—eight times over. Money hadn't changed him. He was still the consummate slob, but his wealth had turned his slovenly habits into fashion.

He didn't argue when I told him I needed him to look after my old man for a few hours. "You bet, Tony. No problem."

We arranged to meet at his new office at the intersection of Ben White and Highway 290.

I dropped off John Roney, a twelve-pack of Old Milwaukee, and a bag of burgers at Jack's with the promise that I would explain it all when I returned. "It might be nothing." I glanced at my watch. "Maybe an hour, maybe two."

He grinned, his pan-shaped face almost cherubic in its innocence. "We'll be here."

As usual, tourists, natives, and drunks jammed Sixth Street; as usual, all parking spaces were filled; so as usual, I pulled into a Loading Zone, rummaged through my stack of magnetized signs I kept behind the seat, retrieved two imprinted with the logo BLEVINS' BREWERY, and stuck one to the outside of the driver's door and one on the passenger's door.

Neon Larry waved at me when I entered. He pointed to the hall leading to the rear of the bar. I nodded and headed back to his office, where I found Goofyfoot lying on Larry's battered couch, his phlegmy eyes staring at me.

He'd been sleeping, but the faint hiss of hinges opening awakened him.

One curious fact I've noticed over the years about the homeless, unless they're drunker than a skunk: you can't slip up on them. There's an animal wariness that comes from living on the edges of society, sleeping in culverts, hiding in cardboard boxes, and taking what you can get when you can get it.

He sat up and grinned.

I sat beside him and pushed twenty bucks in his grimy hand. "What's this about my old man?"

The wizened man frowned. "I heard it from Downtown. Him and me was at the convention center last night. Big shindig dinner. Some of the stuff they throw away ain't never been touched."

Nodding impatiently, I prompted him. "I know. Now what do you have to tell me about my old man?"

"Well, we was talking about Sal and what happened to him. Downtown said three guys talked to him that morning, asking if he knew your pa. When he said he did, they gave him five bucks to tell them where he was. He didn't know except he was staying with you."

I started to ask just how Downtown had learned that John Roney was with me, but then I remembered I had told Goofyfoot. I grinned wryly when I thought of the old saw from when I was a kid, *You don't need a telegraph or telephone, just tell a woman.* Well, that aphorism should be amended to *tell a bum.* Not one piece of information was privileged on the street if it would buy a beer or a burger or a cigarette.

I studied the old man. "So what made Downtown think they were going to do a number on my old man?"

Despite being in a closed room, the slight man leaned forward. "They was the same ones that went after the Butcherman."

Hymie Weinshank!

Suddenly, I remembered earlier that day when the Peterbilt ran us off the road. Maybe that driver wasn't just careless. Maybe he was trying to kill us.

I left the old man in Neon Larry's office and slipped onto a barstool out front. Larry gave me his gap-toothed grin and brushed his long black hair out of his eyes. "Beer?"

"No." I nodded to the coffeepot behind the counter. "Some of that."

"Leaded or unleaded?"

"Leaded."

"Here you go," he said, sliding a thick white mug filled with steaming coffee in front of me. "On the house."

"What do I owe for Goofyfoot?"

He shrugged. "Forget it."

For the next few minutes, I sipped my coffee and sorted through my thoughts.

If Hymie and his boys were the goons who croaked Sal, then they must believe that John Roney could identify them. The only way they could have known about him is if they saw him, which meant he could not have been passed out like Butcherman said, at least not at the time Sal was killed.

I shook my head. The whole scheme didn't make sense. Sure, if Hymie had wasted a public figure, he would have been forced to take care of any witnesses, but a transient, a hobo who drifted from place to place with no attachments? It was a cold fact I always hated to admit, but the death of a transient wasn't accorded much more concern than a dog struck by a car.

Sure, lip service was given and detectives were assigned, but the daily intensity of crime on American streets kept the good guys too busy to worry over a homeless person.

So why go out of their way with my old man? There had to be more at stake than the testimony of an unreliable drunk for Hymie to take a chance on another killing.

I remembered the wild idea that had popped into my head after I spoke with the guards Eddie Borke and Jack Ramsey at Quad-County Armored Car Services, the crazy idea that perhaps Carl Edwards was the one knocked unconscious at the heist, and it was his body Salinas Sal saw being transferred from one car to another that night at Barton Springs.

That, I told myself, would be motive enough to get rid of any eyewitnesses.

On impulse, I pulled out my three-by-five cards and thumbed through them. When I found what I was looking for, I waved Neon Larry over. I shouted above the roar of the crowd. "Telephone directory?"

He pointed to his office.

Goofyfoot was gone, so I slid behind Larry's desk and spread my cards on the desk pad before me. Next to Eddie and Jack's interview, I laid out the cards covering the interview with Frank Cooper.

I wanted to be sure I had not imagined anything.

After rereading the cards, I grinned and looked up the number for Jack Ramsey and Eddie Borke. I had a question for them.

Ramsey didn't answer, but Borke caught it on the third ring. I identified myself. "Sorry to bother you, but I wanted to make sure I understood what happened that day."

"No problem. What do you want to know?"

"Let me read it to you. Here's what I jotted down after our conversation. 'We did hear someone else come in. Jack and me here have talked about it. Someone came in and said something like 'what' or something, and then there was a thud and someone fell to the floor. For a couple of minutes, you could hear them coming and going, and then there was a gunshot, and the door slammed shut." I paused. "That sound right?"

"Yeah. Sure."

"Now let me ask you this question, Eddie."

"Shoot." He hesitated, and then sheepishly added, "No pun intended."

I laughed. "No problem. Now, when you and Jack were lying on the floor, did you hear one of the—no, anyone shout, lay down or I'll shoot?"

He pondered the question a moment. "No. We could hardly make out what they were saying. We heard a groan and something or somebody fall to the floor, and then a minute or two later, the shot." He hesitated. "I ain't saying them words weren't said, but I sure don't remember them."

After hanging up, I sat staring at the receiver while the wheels in my brain whirled. I'd come up with the most cockamamy theory in my entire career. One that might get me fired or killed, or both.

Chapter Twenty

I glanced at my watch. It was late, almost 11:00. I wanted to bounce my ideas off Marty, but no telling where he was. I knew one place he wasn't, and that was home, which was the last place I would call for him.

Climbing back in my Chevy Silverado, I drove around aimlessly for a few minutes, doing my best to find some sort of sanity in my thoughts.

The overwhelming belief that someone other than Carl Edwards masterminded the heist swept over me, too strong for me to ignore.

But, I told myself, if I truly believed that theory, then I had to believe that Frank Cooper was lying.

I pulled up to a red light and stopped. I asked myself, why would he lie?

Simple, you dummy. He was the architect of the scheme. But why? What was his motive? I shook my head, unwilling to commit myself to such preposterous conjecture and, at the same time, cursing the cyberspace snafu that had cut me off from Eddie Dyson.

I had to be certain, but how?

Cooper had been shot, close range as he said. His shirt was powder-burned. On the other hand, I told myself, he was the only witness. The entire case hinged on his credibility, which I had to admit appeared to be beyond question.

So far!

Then I remembered my interview with Rita Johnson, which threw cold water on my cockamamy theory. Maybe that was all it was, a half-baked idea, for Rita told me Carl Edwards had spoken of a fishing trip to New Mexico and of a small village named Lost Lake.

Could he be there? It was too early in the season for trout. The only reason he would be there was if he were hiding out. And if he were, then that was the ball game. One, two, three strikes, and he was out.

But, if he weren't—

Behind me a horn blared. I jerked back to the present and saw the green light before me. I sped away, at the same time knowing I had to take a trip to Lost Lake, wherever it was in the rugged mountains of New Mexico.

But first, I needed to make suitable arrangements for my old man. If the little ideas bubbling in the back of my head all came together, John Roney Boudreaux might very well need protection.

And there was no one to whom I would turn other than Danny O'Banion.

"No sweat, Tony, boy. We'll look after your old man," Danny said. He hooked a thumb at a couple of his soldiers. One nodded. "They'll pick him up now and bring him back."

"Thanks." I gave him Jack Edney's address.

He grew serious. "You want me to send someone with you? That's lonesome country up there in New Mexico, I hear."

I grinned and shook my head. "Thanks, but no thanks. You and your boys will have your hands full with my old man. I'll stop by the D.A.'s before I leave and tell Mark he'll be with you." I paused and grinned. "That is, unless you don't want to rub shoulders with the District Attorney's office."

He laughed, all the freckles on his face running into one big splotch. "Hey, why should I mind? I'm as legit as there is in this town." He grew serious. "You sure about this, Tony? You're not stretching it, are you?"

With a groan, I closed my eyes and squeezed my nose and mouth with one hand. "I hope not. This whole thing is like a spiderweb. It could fall apart. If I find Carl Edwards in New Mexico, I'll know my little theories were just that, theories not worth the paper they were written on." I drew a deep breath. "To be honest, Danny, I trust that man as much as I trust you. I can't imagine he would pull a heist like that. That's why I'm crossing my fingers that I don't find him at Lost Lake."

After touching base with Marty, I called the District Attorney's office. Investigator Mark Swain's answering machine picked up my call. I told him where my old man would be. Then I called Janice to tell her I would be out of town the next day instead of at the auto show.

While she assured me she understood the situation, the cool snippiness in her responses told me I'd be forced to do a great deal of groveling when I returned.

Finally, at 2:00 A.M., after locating the village of Lost Lake some fifty miles northeast of Santa Fe, New Mexico, I caught a flight that touched down in Dallas/Fort Worth, and then made a two-hour layover in Amarillo before continuing to Santa Fe.

In an almost deserted coffee shop with online facilities at Rick Husband Amarillo International, I sat hunched over a cup of lukewarm coffee studying my notes.

I'm not the sharpest knife in the PI business, but I've learned that perseverance and attention to detail pay off in the long run. It seemed as if every time I reread my notes, I noticed a link I had failed to recognize earlier.

I reread the notes of my first interview with Margaret Edwards. When I asked her if her husband had ever mentioned a fishing trip to Falcon Reservoir, "Not a word" was her response.

After studying the card another moment, I started to put it away, but then a thought hit me.

Quickly I thumbed through the notes until I found my interview with Frank Cooper. I skimmed the notes when I saw that my memory had served me well, for I had mentioned Falcon to him.

A tiny bell rang in the back of my mind. I closed my eyes, trying to force the tenuous thought into a firm idea. Then I remembered. Rita Johnson had mentioned Falcon. Lake Falcon, she called it.

I leaned back and stared, unseeing, out the expansive windows at the taxiing jets. How did she know about Falcon? Edwards had not even mentioned it to his wife. And other than her and Debbie, the only one I'd told was Frank Cooper. Could there be some kind of connection between Cooper and Johnson?

Pulling out my laptop, I connected to the airport's Wi-Fi and tried to e-mail Eddie Dyson again. To my disgust, cyberspace still refused to give up his address.

Shaking my head, I logged off and returned to my note cards. Moments later, my flight was announced.

By now the sun was rising over the flat Texas prairie that stretched farther to the west than the eye could see. As the thirty-seat Embraer 120 Brasilia jet climbed into the cloudless sky, I leaned back and gazed out the window, grateful that I was sitting by myself. I would have made a lousy traveling companion, for I was too busy trying to fit pieces into my little theory that Frank Cooper was behind the heist.

Of course, I had no motive. There was opportunity and means, but half of the credit union employees had opportunity and means.

Shuffling my note cards, I studied his interview, hoping to find something that would bring into question his credibility. Anyone could have worn a herringbone jacket, and at least two or three of those I had questioned were of his stature.

At the next words I'd written, my heart leaped into my throat. *I recognized his voice.*

Pulse racing, I riffled through the cards to my notes for the interview with Eddie Borke and Jack Ramsey, the Quad-County Armored Car Service's guards. To one of my questions, Eddie had replied, "One thing I remember about the voice, though, is that it sounded kind of raspy."

I had prompted him. "Like laryngitis, maybe?"

And then the two guards had looked at each other and nodded simultaneously. "Yeah, like laryngitis," replied Eddie.

Staring up at the overhead, I concentrated. Someone else had mentioned laryngitis, someone at the credit union. Romero? Elizabeth Romero?

I was so excited, I spilled the note cards in my lap. Agitated at my own clumsiness, I gathered them and fumbled for the interview with Elizabeth Romero, Raiford Lindsey's executive secretary.

A young flight attendant with a concerned look on her face stopped at my side. "Are you all right, sir?" She glanced at the cards strewn over my lap and on the floor. "Can I help?"

I forced a laugh. "No, thanks. I can do it. Just clumsy. Serves me right."

Finally, after what seemed like hours, I found the card I was searching for. I skimmed it. There it is, I shouted to myself as I read her remark. "He could barely talk with laryngitis that day because he was wheezing and hacking from a bad cold."

Leaning back, I stared out the window, wondering what to do next. I had two witnesses with contradictory testimony regarding Edwards' voice that day. Or did I?

Muttering to myself, I realized that Cooper could very well have recognized Edwards' raspy voice. And perhaps in his fear, he thought Edwards was shouting.

I shook my head and groaned, hoping I was not permitting my personal feelings to interfere with my investigation.

My thoughts drifted back to Rita Johnson and Lake Falcon. Perhaps Edwards had mentioned it to her. Maybe this was another instance of where I was giving in to my personal feelings.

And then I remembered her last joking remark, "Maybe it was because we were both southpaws."

For a fleeting moment I froze, stunned.

Chapter Twenty-one

I reread that note card half a dozen times, all the while cursing my own stupidity. A southpaw? A lefty?

Yet, Frank Cooper had been shot in the left side, not the right side, the side that would be facing a left-handed gunman.

Closing my eyes, I leaned back against the seat and tried to steady my nerves. I couldn't believe I had overlooked these pieces of information for the last few days.

I was comfortable around firearms, having grown up with them and, from time to time, relying on them in extreme cases in my job.

And I knew of no one who did not use his dominant hand when handling a handgun, be it a .357 magnum or a .22 popgun. That meant, I told myself, that if Carl Edwards had fired the shot that struck Cooper in the side, the wound would have been on Cooper's right side, not left.

A flashing sign above the closed door to the cockpit signaled passengers to buckle up. Hastily, I jammed the cards back in my pocket and followed instructions.

The pilot came over the intercom, announcing that weather was forcing us to divert to Albuquerque.

From the porthole window, I saw a light snow dusting the ground, an ominous portent of what possibly lay ahead.

* * *

I shivered as I headed across the street to the Enchantment Auto Rental. The dispatcher, a weary-eyed lady in wool slacks and a bulky wool sweater informed me that before I reached Santa Fe, I might need to fit the tire chains to the Ford Taurus I was renting. She paused, glanced at the credit information I had provided and, with a crooked grin, said, "You know how to put them on, don't you?"

I grinned sheepishly. "We don't have much use for snow chains down in Austin, Texas, ma'am."

She chuckled. "About ten miles this side of Santa Fe, pull into the Golden Globe Truck Stop. If you need them, they'll take care of it for you." She eyed my clothing. "To be honest, friend, you best pop across the street at Target or Academy Outdoors and get some proper gear. The temperature drops like a lead balloon up them mountains. You'll freeze your lanky tail off."

Thirty minutes later, after putting over four hundred bucks on my VISA card, I headed up I-25 North. The snowfall remained light, but the gusting wind blew it sideways, forcing me to keep the wipers moving.

It was just after 10:00, but the ponderous gray clouds lumbering across the mountains made it seem like dusk. The warm air from the heater felt good.

About halfway to Santa Fe, the snow stopped falling, and to my surprise, back to the west the clouds broke. According to the FM station I was listening to, no snow was expected for a couple of days. I muttered a short prayer of thanks, at the same time remembering the shaky prognostications of our local weathermen back home.

In Santa Fe, I bypassed the truck stop and pulled into a restaurant for a hot lunch.

* * *

From Santa Fe, I headed northeast, higher into the Sangre de Cristo Mountains before, about mid-afternoon, I dropped down into the Santa Fe Basin, which was where I spotted Mount Baldy.

According to my directions, Lost Lake, a one-time gold mining town that had turned to tourism, sat on the eastern slope of Baldy.

It was from my *Grand-père* Moise that I picked up my appreciation for the beauty and complexity of nature. Even on the desolate Louisiana prairies and back in the forbidding swamps, there was grandeur about if you wanted to see it.

When I rounded the last bend in the highway and looked down upon the small village of Lost Lake, I was awestruck by its simple beauty. It was Christmas-card perfect, with its snow-laden roofs and rustic buildings with golden lights shining from store windows.

Perhaps a dozen shops lined either side of the highway that continued its sinuous route higher into the mountains. There was little traffic, which I guessed was to be expected this time of year, although I noted several snow-covered slopes around the village.

There were a couple of motels, the closest being the Ski Slope. I pulled up to the wooden hitching rail in front of the office. When I opened the car door, the bitter cold drove into my bones. I shivered and slammed the door without getting out, grabbing the heavy parka that had set me back over a hundred bucks, but when I opened the door again, it was worth the money. Except for my hands and face, I was as warm as the proverbial piece of toast.

Once inside, I discovered that while the exterior of the motel might appear rustic, the interior was snug and cozy, with central heating spewing out warm air. Adjoining the lobby was a spacious lounge where a handful of individuals were basking in the heat from a blazing fireplace and enjoying a belly-warming libation.

A beaming old man who had to be in his eighties grinned when I hurried in and slammed the door behind me. "Welcome, friend. Get in here and burn the chill out of your bones."

I asked for a room, and he chuckled, his wind-burned cheeks wrinkling with a wry grin. "This time of year, we got 'em to spare. Season's about over." He slipped me a registration card and nodded to the few men and women milling about in the lounge. "They're the last of the diehards, hanging in until the last bit of snow is history."

Cocking his head so he could read my name, he asked, "Be staying long, Mr. Boudreaux? That's French, ain't it?"

I grinned to myself when he pronounced the name Boo-dru-x. "Yep. Louisiana, but I live in Austin, Texas now."

He shot his slender arm across the counter. "Name's Willie Morales. I own this place. Happy to know you."

I slid the registration card back to him, and along with it, a snapshot of Carl Edwards. "Thanks." I paused, and then continued, nodding to the snapshot. "I'm trying to find this gent. He's missing, and his wife and daughter are worried. He mentioned fishing up here in Lost Lake."

Willie grunted. "Ain't no fishing up here this time of year," he muttered, staring at the snapshot for several seconds before shaking his head. "Nope. Don't recognize the fella. If he came up here often, he might of stayed down at the Dunes. That's the other motel in town."

"Good enough." I nodded to my registration. "I'll probably be here a couple nights at least."

After dropping off my gear in my room, which was snug

and warm, I headed out, planning on working my way down one side of the street to the Dunes Motel, and back up the other side.

Next door to the Ski Slope Motel was a brightly lit liquor store. I gave the clerk the same story, and he gave me the same answer. "What about the name Carl Edwards? Ever hear that?"

He gestured to the snapshot. "That this feller's name?"

"Yeah."

"Sorry."

As I reached for the door, he stopped me. "Tell you who might know. Abner Sweet. He's across the street at Mountain Realtors. A lot of rich folks own summer homes around here and rent them out in the winter. Abner handles a lot of them. Then down the street at Pure Creek Real Estate is Myrtle Cummings. She rents a lot of them too. Maybe one of them has heard of this old boy."

By now, it was dark. The clouds had blown away, and the frosty night seemed to enhance the brilliance of the stars sparkling down on the small village.

I caught Abner Sweet as the rotund man was locking up his business for the night. He held the snapshot in the glow of lights from the saloon next door. "Nope. Never seen the man."

"What about the name Carl Edwards? Ever hear that?"

He pursed his thick lips. "Hmm. Edwards, Edwards. I know some Edwards, but no one named Carl." He handed me the picture. "Sorry."

"Thanks anyway. Oh, by the way, can you point me toward the Pure Creek Real Estate? The clerk at the Mountain Top Liquor store told me Myrtle Cummings might be able to help if you couldn't."

He chuckled. "She might, but you won't find her at the

office this time of night." He pointed down and across the street to the garish lights of the Mount Baldy Bar and Grill.

The lights reflected green and red off the snow. "That's where you'll find her. Can't miss her. Skinny as a rail with short hair, almost white."

Thanking him, I stepped off the sidewalk, paused as a car passed, and then slogged through the melting snow to the bar, grateful I had ponied up the money to buy some waterproof boots. My running shoes would have been no match for the slop I waded through.

Myrtle Cummings was a snap to spot. Perched on a bar stool, she was chatting amiably with a gent wearing an overcoat and a western hat tipped to the back of his head.

Apologizing for interrupting her, I gave her the same story I'd given the others, and she gave me the same answer after studying the snapshot. "Nope. He don't look familiar." She showed it to the rancher next to her. "You recognize him, Finas?"

The wiry cowpoke shook his head. "Nope." He handed it to a woman a couple of barstools away. "What about it, Connie? You seen this feller around?"

Connie was a tad overweight. She shifted about on the stool, held the snapshot up to the dim light and, after several moments, shook her head. "Never seen him." She held out the picture to me.

I continued as I retrieved the snapshot. "He goes by the name Carl Edwards."

To my surprise, Myrtle Cummings nodded. "Carl Edwards? Why, I rented him the Carmony place up near the lake a few days ago."

Chapter Twenty-two

The unexpected announcement hit me between the eyes, exploding my little theories like a hundred-megaton bomb.

Carl Edwards was alive. That meant that he indeed had masterminded the heist and had picked this isolated part of the country in which to disappear.

I frowned, wondering where he had been in the weeks since the heist. "A few days, you say?"

"Yeah. But it wasn't this guy in the picture. His name was—" She paused, wrinkling her forehead in concentration. "Let's see, Irwin, Charles Irwin. Real skinny. He rented it for this Carl Edwards guy. Paid cash for a month in advance."

Irwin? The name meant nothing to me. "He was by himself?"

"No. There was another gentleman in the car out front. Mr. Irwin said this Edwards was a writer and needed someplace secluded."

Finas chuckled. "Ain't no place no more secluded than the Carmony place."

She shrugged and grinned at her friend. "You ever hear of a writer named Edwards, Finas?"

Finas shrugged. "You know better'n that, Myrt! I never read nothing except the comics."

Myrtle laughed. "Anyway, that's what he said."

"You seen him back in town since?"

She pondered my question. "Not really. Saw him drive through a couple of days back with two other fellas. They didn't stop. Just headed on out to the Carmony place."

"Carmony place, huh? How do I get there?"

She gave me directions that were so convoluted I knew I had to wait until morning. A couple of the turn-offs marked by nothing more than fallen pines or deserted sheds would be too easy to miss in the dark. With the temperature plummeting, I didn't want to get stuck out all night.

The small village might have been out of the way, but it had all the modern conveniences that appeal to tourists: satellite TV, central heat, and Wi-Fi.

That night, I pulled up my e-mail and, with mixed feelings, discovered that cyberspace had decided to play ball. Meekly it handed over Eddie Dyson's response to my inquiries concerning Raiford Lindsey and Frank Cooper. Go figure.

Both men were in hock from the top of their heads to the soles of their feet. And then some.

I printed out his report and settled back on the couch to peruse the information. I couldn't help whistling in surprise as I skimmed the report. Of the two, Cooper appeared to be on shakier financial ground.

Lindsey had taken out options on several thousand acres in South Texas on either side of a proposed toll road from Mexico to the Texas Panhandle that the Texas governor was trying to dump on the Texas taxpayers. Lindsey had a one-hundred-thousand-dollar note due in two months.

According to Eddie, Cooper was a silent partner in Golden Gate Oil Brokers Incorporated, which had for the last several months been under fire from federal investigators because of deceptive accounting, including hiding various manipulative practices that enhanced profitability reports for stockholders and the government.

Now, I'm not too astute on most business practices, but over the years I've seen companies literally rip the financial belly from hundreds of thousands of average investors simply because of greed.

Fortunately, some of those responsible received well-deserved prison terms, but even that satisfaction was a moot point to those who lost their life savings or had their retirements wiped out.

Both Lindsey and Cooper now had motive. Both had opportunity. Both had means. But, I reminded myself, Carl Edwards was purportedly here, alive.

So much for Cooper's or Lindsey's motives.

Still, I couldn't help toying with various scenarios.

Remembering Eddie Borke and Jack Ramsey's sketchy description of the heist men, I could eliminate Raiford Lindsey. The two guards stated the gunmen were about their size, which was slender, not bowling-ball round like Raiford Lindsey.

That left Cooper, of whom several questions continued to nag at me. Unfortunately, there was a plausible explanation for each.

He claimed to have recognized Edwards' voice, but the slight vice president had laryngitis. Maybe it was the hoarseness he recognized.

Second, the gunshot wound Cooper suffered was to his left side, the side opposite where a southpaw would likely have fired if the two were standing face to face. To be fair, Edwards might not have been standing directly in front of Cooper, which meant he could have shot Cooper in the left side.

And third, other than Edwards' family, Cooper was the only one I mentioned Falcon Reservoir to, yet the next day, Rita Johnson suggested the lake. Was he the one who told Rita about it? If so, why? Or had Carl Edwards told her in casual conversation? That, though, was too much of a stretch. He had never even mentioned it to his own wife.

I stared, unseeing, at the TV. Despite knowing Carl Edwards was alive, I couldn't shake the feeling I was working on a puzzle with half a dozen pieces missing. And without those pieces, I'd never learn the truth.

During the night, I awakened every time the heating unit kicked in, which was frequently. I discovered why when I glanced at the sliding glass doors the next morning and saw nothing but the artistic handiwork of Jack Frost scribbled across the glass.

I slid a door open, and the bitter air took my breath away. I slammed it quickly and whistled. Donning my wool trousers and shirt, I slipped into the fur-lined boots and stomped downstairs to the motel lounge where flames leaped in the massive fireplace, sending their warmth around the room to the handful of customers enjoying their breakfast.

On a highboy against one wall was a continental buffet, so I helped myself to a cup of steaming coffee and a cinnamon bagel. A couple sat in front of the blazing fire.

One or two motel guests nodded to me, and I returned their greeting.

"Cold enough for you?" one sunburned man asked with an amiable grin.

I shivered and slid onto the couch in front of the fire. "Too cold."

"Where you from?"

"Austin."

He chuckled. "Gets a tad colder up here, friend. Twenty degrees this morning."

I laughed with him. "I'm finding that out."

At that moment, the proprietor, Willie Morales, came through. He pulled up when he spotted me. "Any luck finding your gent?"

"I'm not sure. Myrtle Cummings said a guy by that name rented the Carmony place. I'm driving up there this morning."

He clicked his tongue and gave his head a shake. "Narrow roads up through there. Almost deserted. Lucky if two jeeps a week go through. You watch yourself." He studied my clothing from head to foot. "Looks like you're dressed okay. Got a parka and gloves?"

His remark puzzled me. "Yeah. I'm only going to be gone a couple of hours."

The man next to me wearing a bulky turtleneck sweater leaned forward and extended his hand. "They call me Norby Collins. I own the gun shop down the street. I don't mean to butt in, but it wouldn't hurt if you took some emergency gear with you." When I frowned, he continued. "Likely as not, you'll not need it, but weather up here is mighty fickle. Never hurts to have something to fall back on if worse comes to worst and you can't make it back in tonight."

I glanced up at Willie. He nodded. "Norby's right, Mr. Boudreaux." This time he pronounced my name correctly. "Sometimes two hours can turn into two days."

I patted my pocket. "No cell phone service up here?"

Both men chuckled. "That's the beauty of this place," Willie said.

Norby leaned back, a grin on his ruddy face. "Come on by my place, Mr. Boudreaux. I keep a couple of backpacks put together with poncho shelters, mini warmers, dried food,

Thermo-Lite blanket, medical kit, and fire starters. I'll toss one in your car. If you don't use it, just drop it off when you come back."

I lifted an eyebrow at the hospitable offer. "Sounds fair enough to me."

"And," Willie added, "best you put chains on them wheels."

Thirty minutes later, tire chains, emergency pack, and all, I pulled out, heading north up into the pine- and fir-covered slopes of the rugged Sangre de Cristo Mountains. Snow still lay in the shady slopes and crevices of the mountain.

I grinned when I remembered how Norby Collins had insisted I stash a few envelopes of dehydrated food and food bars as well as a fire starter in my parka. In fact, after demonstrating its use, he had fastened a small starter to the zipper tab on my coat. He started to explain, but I beat him to it. "I know, I know. Never can tell what might happen."

He had laughed. "You learn fast, Mr. Boudreaux."

The first few miles, the drive was everything a travel agent could say about the mountains. Tall pines, bushy firs, various understory vegetation growing around the rocky boulders lining the narrow road, which was not much more than a couple of ruts over rocky slopes. On either side of the bumpy road, icy streams sluiced down the mountainside, their swift moving water cutting through banks of snow.

My first turnoff sent me climbing steeper up the slope. From time to time, the road switched back, climbing slowly, and at each switchback, the road widened, leaving ample space for vehicles to park as others made their way up or down.

The slopes between the switchbacks were vast fields of small boulders, black and gray, covered with patches of lichen and moss. A sudden motion in one of the fields caught my attention. I braked to a halt and stared at the sprawling carpet of various size stones.

Suddenly, a tiny marmot darted from under one stone to another and then a bird that reminded me of a Bob White quail shot out and zoomed across the field of boulders.

The little marmot vanished.

Taking my foot off the brake, I continued up the road.

There were no guardrails along the precipitous slopes, so I kept as close to the middle of the road as possible, crossing my fingers I wouldn't meet anyone coming down and thankful I'd had chains put on the car.

The fallen snow seemed to be lying in thicker patches. The temperature grew cooler, and I kicked up the heat in the Ford Taurus.

Suddenly, a deer darted across the road, followed by a second one. I slammed on the brakes and watched as they clambered up the rocky slope.

Drawing a deep breath and releasing it slowly, I continued climbing until I reached the last turnoff, a narrow trail marked by a crumbling cabin. I was about twenty minutes out of Lost Lake by now.

The slope was steep, so steep, I shifted down into a lower drive and crept upward. I thought to myself that whoever owned this place must have four-wheel drive, for I doubted my rented Taurus' automatic transmission could take the strain of such a climb too often.

The narrow road switched back several times, each about fifty feet above the other. After another ten minutes of winding through a forest of skyscraping pines and bushy firs and gently easing around the sharp switchbacks, I drove onto a rocky plateau some hundred yards wide, covered with patches of snow. I braked to a halt. At the back of the granite plate, a sprawling, two-story log cabin sat at the base of the mountain slope. A Cadillac was parked in front.

I whistled softly. The place was the epitome of isolation. I had the feeling the Carmonys didn't care for drop-in visitors.

For a few moments, I studied the cabin, my stomach churning with anticipation of what lay ahead. If Edwards was here, I didn't want to find him. I chided myself for letting my own feelings become involved, yet I couldn't help it.

Tendrils of smoke rose lazily from chimneys at either end of the house, and the soft purr of a generator drifted through the air.

Taking a deep breath, I eased forward, wondering just what I would say to Carl Edwards if I came face to face with him. And what would he say to me?

Would he attempt to keep me from revealing his whereabouts? If so, how? I couldn't imagine his resorting to extreme measures to keep me quiet. He might be many things, but he was no killer. Yet, allegedly he shot Frank Cooper.

All I could do was shake my head as I pulled up to the sprawling cabin and climbed out of the Taurus.

I climbed the stairs to the porch running the length of the sprawling cabin. I couldn't help admiring the structure. It was one of those you would expect to see in a national magazine or TV program.

Halting in front of two massive slab doors, I pounded the heavy brass knocker.

Moments later, the door opened, and a slender man, about six feet or so, faced me. "Yes?" His voice was high-pitched and thin.

I glanced past his shoulder into the cavernous room and said, "I'm Tony Boudreaux. I was told a Mr. Carl Edwards had rented this house."

His large eyes stared at me from his sepulcher face. "So?"

"So," I replied, sticking an unfelt grin on my face, "I'd like to see him if he doesn't mind. His wife sent me," I added.

The last remark got his attention. "Oh. I beg your pardon, Mr. Boudreaux. Certainly. This way, if you please."

Though his voice sent shivers up my spine, I was pleasantly surprised at the sudden cooperation. I stepped inside and followed him across a shiny floor of heartwood pine. I couldn't help noticing he wore a light sport coat over a pair of lightweight slacks. He was as new to the mountains as I was.

To one side, a fire blazed in a fireplace constructed of the granite rocks from the surrounding slopes. Chairs and couches covered with Navajo blankets faced the fire. The blankets were red with white, blue, yellow, and green horizontal stripes with spider woman crosses.

He halted in front of an ornately carved slab door and knocked. From inside came a voice. "Yes?"

"A visitor, sir. A Mr. Boudreaux from Austin, Texas."

I stiffened. How did he know I was from Austin?

"Show him in."

The tall angular man opened the door and ushered me inside.

I nodded to him as I passed, and then jerked to a halt, staring into the leering face of Hymie Weinshank!

Chapter Twenty-three

Sitting with his back to the blazing fire in the rock fire-place, Weinshank sneered. "Come in, Mr. Boudreaux. We've been waiting for you."

To say I was stunned would be an understatement of the same magnitude as saying Noah's flood was a passing shower. I had been flimflammed, fooled, faked out, and like a country bumpkin, I'd walked right into it. I tried to cover my confusion. "I beg your pardon? I didn't know I was expected."

From an adjoining room came Alex White, wearing a sneer on his face that put Hymie's to shame. That meant the one with the face of a skeleton had to be Maury Erickson. I glanced at Alex, who also wore lightweight clothing, then frowned down at Hymie.

Weinshank nodded. "Oh, yes, you've been expected. You've been sticking your nose in business that doesn't concern you. We got you up here so we can make sure you don't stick it in nobody else's business," he said, his voice icy with menace.

My mind racing, I glanced around into the hard face of Maury Erickson and grinned at him before turning back to Hymie. I tried to put just the right amount of belligerence into my reply. "To be honest, mister, I don't know you or your friends, and I haven't the remotest idea what you're talking about. I came up here to see Carl Edwards, not to cause any problems. His family asked me to find him. That's the only reason I'm here."

My answer was the chilling click on a hammer being cocked on a handgun. I looked around into the muzzle of a .44 magnum revolver. It really looked like a .900 magnum except they don't make them that size, but at the moment, you couldn't have proven it by me.

"Let me do him now, Hymie," said Maury in his thin, almost ghostlike whisper.

Hymie studied me a few moments, crossing one leg over the other. I saw that he wore low-cut slippers. Apparently, none of the three planned on staying around long enough to dress for the weather.

Keeping his black eyes on mine, he grinned. "No. Not here. I got a feeling Mr. Boudreaux nosed around down in Lost Lake enough that citizens there know he's up here. Ain't that right?"

I pretended to play dumb, but I didn't have to pretend to play scared. I was. "Look, Hymie—is that your name? What's going on here? I'm just a poor slob trying to earn a buck by running down a missing husband, that's all." I tried to laugh, but the chuckle caught in my throat. "That's no reason to kill someone."

Alex White laughed. "He's a cool one, Hymie." He took a couple of steps toward me and sneered. "Yeah, you might be cool, buddy, but you can't hide that black eye or that knot on your head. Remember him, Hymie? He was out at the Zuider Zee and Bernie's Crab Shack last week when someone was spying on us."

Hymie nodded slowly, a smug grin on his face. "I remember. I recognized him right off."

I played along with them. "Yeah. I was there. Edwards

was supposed to hang out at the Zuider Zee. I dropped by, didn't see him, then went over to Bernie's for supper. What's the crime in that?"

"Ain't no crime. Just stupid," growled Hymie.

"Yeah," Alex chimed in. "I bet he's the one what knocked me into the river." He took another step forward and pulled an automatic. "I ought—"

Hymie snapped. "You ain't oughta do nothing."

Alex hesitated, the hate blazing in his eyes obvious.

I tried another tack. Holding my hands out to my side in supplication, I said, "Look, fellas. You got this all wrong. This is one crazy coincidence. Yeah, I was out there where you say, but I didn't spy on no one, and I sure didn't kick someone in the river." As soon as the word "kick" rolled off my lips, I cringed, hoping no one had caught the slip of tongue.

As usual, I was wrong.

Hymie's eyes narrowed in triumph. "Nobody said nothing about kicking, Mr. Boudreaux. The only way you could have known that is if you was down there that night."

Alex frowned, failing to comprehend Hymie's explanation. Then his watery eyes lit with understanding. "Hey, yeah. That's right." He raised his automatic over his head as if to club me. "You dirty—"

"Alex!" Hymie's cold voice stopped the larger man in his tracks. "Not here. I don't want no blood anywhere around here. I don't want no chance of them bluebirds finding any kind of DNA out here." He gestured to the door. "Put him in his car."

I knew now I couldn't convince them I was nothing more than an innocent PI searching for a missing man. I had no one to blame but myself, but still, I played for time, trying to figure out my next move. Once they got me in the car, my goose was baked and basted better than any Christmas dinner.

"All right, all right." I drew a deep breath and released it slowly. With what I hoped was an appropriate degree of resignation, I asked, "At least tell me what happened to Carl Edwards."

All three laughed. Hymie nodded to Maury behind me. In his thin voice, he chuckled and replied, "Don't worry. You'll be meeting up with him before long."

I stared at Hymie. "He's dead?"

Pursing his lips, Hymie sneered. "Give the man a blue ribbon. At the bottom of a canyon along with his car."

Maury leered. "Yeah. At the bottom of Copper Canyon."

Suddenly, everything fell into place. "You were the ones Sal saw transferring the body out at the park."

Hymie's scarred face twisted in a frown. Alex explained, "Sal was that wino down at the train yard. You remember."

"Oh, that one. Yeah. I remember."

I took a wild guess, although it was not as wild as it would have been a few minutes earlier. "Frank Cooper planned it, and when Edwards stumbled in, Cooper knocked him out, and shot himself. You threw Edwards in the armored car, then transferred him to your car at the warehouse downtown where you killed him."

Nodding his square head and grinning in appreciation, Hymie laughed. "You ain't so dumb after all."

Alex snorted. "Dumb enough to get hisself whacked."

"Yeah, but there's been a lot of marks dumber." His face went cold. "Search him. See if he's packing heat."

From behind, Maury patted me down, pausing at the envelopes of dried food in my parka, and then dismissing them. He paid no attention to the fire starter on my zipper tab, and to tell the truth, at the time, neither did I.

Maury backed away. "He's clean, Hymie."

"Put him in his car. Alex, you drive with Boudreaux in front. Maury, you sit in the back. This joker moves a muscle, blow his stinking head off."

Maury's watery eyes filled with a gleam of perverted excitement. "Can I do him, Hymie, huh? Can I do him?"

Alex shook his head and shrugged.

"Sure, Maury," replied Hymie. "But not until I say so."

Maury grabbed me by the arm and pushed me toward the door. "Let's go, Boudreaux."

As quickly as one scheme popped into my head, it popped out again. I couldn't break and run. All three had pieces. They'd nail me before I made ten feet. Same as outside. For a moment, I considered shoving one into another as we headed down the steps, creating enough confusion so I could dash to the end of the porch and disappear into the forest above the cabin.

I paused when we stepped onto the porch, ostensibly to zip my parka, at the same time gauging the distance to the end of the porch. About a hundred feet. A long, long, long hundred feet. There were a few chairs I could yank behind me, possibly deflecting or throwing off their aim.

Alex gave me a shove. "Don't worry about zipping up. In a few minutes, you ain't going to feel the cold no way."

Hymie spoke up. "Hold it right there."

We froze.

He stepped past us and down the steps. At the base, he turned and held his automatic on me. "Now, come on down, boys."

"What's up, Hymie?" Alex asked.

"Nothing. It's just I got the feeling Boudreaux here has something up his sleeve, and I ain't going to give him a chance to play it. Now, come on down."

I muttered a string of curses under my breath. Another option blown. Behind me, Maury gave me a shove. "You heard the man, Boudreaux. Get on down."

Hymie waved the muzzle of his automatic at my rental car. "Get behind the wheel, Alex. Once they get in, lock the windows and doors from your side. You, Boudreaux, climb in the passenger's side. Maury, you get in behind him while I hold my gun on him. Keep yours cocked. He makes one move, waste him. Understand?"

"Yeah, yeah, Hymie. I understand."

Moments later, I closed the door. Alex locked both it and the window. Only then did Hymie lower his handgun. He went around to the driver's side and spoke to Alex. "I found a spot a couple of miles from here where we can dump him and the car. Nobody will find them for a few weeks." He paused and glanced up at the dark clouds. "And if we get lucky and it snows hard, he might stay covered for months."

As if in answer to Hymie's remark, light flakes of snow started falling from the forbidding sky.

Chapter Twenty-four

Hymie laughed. "What do you know? Look at that. Snowing. We must be living right."

While the irony of his remark was not lost on me, I was too busy trying to lay out another plan, keeping in mind that a skeletal lunatic with a cocked magnum was sitting directly behind me, the muzzle of that cannon no more than mere inches from my skull.

Alex started the car, and then glanced over at me. "Buckle up."

I looked at him in disbelief. "What?"

He nodded to the seat belt. "I said buckle up."

"Why? You're going to kill me in a few minutes anyway."

"Because," Maury growled from behind me, "the road is steep, and if you start bouncing around, I'll blow your head off just like Hymie said."

I buckled up.

"Here we go," Alex announced, pulling in behind Hymie in the Cadillac.

"Don't get too close to Hymie," muttered Maury from the backseat.

"I know what I'm doing," Alex snapped. "Just do your job and leave me alone."

We headed down the steep road to the secondary road, slowly easing around the switchbacks.

"Easy," muttered Maury. "You're too close to the edge of the road."

"Shut up," Alex shouted over his shoulder without taking his eyes off the narrow road.

"The snow's getting thicker," Maury announced.

"I see it, I see it."

Mentally, I crossed my fingers, not wanting to take a chance on any kind of overt movement, for Maury was obviously on edge. I kept my left hand at my side, ready to release the seat belt at a second's notice.

As Hymie slowed for a switchback, a deer suddenly burst across the road just behind the Cadillac. Alex slammed on the brakes, throwing us all forward.

I punched the release button and hurled myself backward, spinning my shoulders and swinging my elbow around. I felt the point of it slam into Maury's skull. At the same time, I jammed my foot on the accelerator, sending the Taurus hurtling forward, slamming into the rear of the Cadillac and sending it careening over the switchback and down the steep slope of rocky talus with us right behind.

Bouncing over the rocks jostled us around like Ping-Pong balls in a bingo machine. In the backseat, Maury was cursing and tumbling about, scrabbling to find the magnum bouncing from door to door.

Scooting around in the seat, I drove both feet into Alex, slamming him against the door, which burst open. With a terrified scream, he tumbled out, and I was right behind him.

Fortunately, he cushioned my fall, although I picked up a couple more knots on my head. I clambered to my feet and scrambled for the forest.

Just before the two vehicles shuddered to a halt on the road below, I reached the forest. I paused to look back, and the boom of a handgun exploded across the slope. A chunk of bark and wood the size of my fist ripped out of the pine beside my head.

The snow grew heavier.

I ran. Behind me, I heard excited voices.

I paused a moment, crouching beside a pine and listening for their shouts. Then, trying to avoid leaving tracks, I headed down the mountain, from time to time stumbling over the tangle of wild grape vines along the edges of clearings. I figured I could find a stream somewhere, and perhaps follow it to civilization, if I could survive Hymie and his boys and the weather.

I heard the crashing of their pursuit behind me.

I lost track of time, but in the mountains, dark comes early and with it the chilling cold of night. The average low temperature in March was in the mid-twenties. At least, I told myself, I'm dressed for it, grateful I had taken the advice of those back in Santa Fe and Lost Lake.

I was still heading down the mountain slope, but with the light quickly fading, I started searching for some shelter out of the cold.

Abruptly, I jerked to a halt, standing on the rim of a twenty-foot drop-off. The hair on the back of my neck tingled. Another step and— I shook my head. I didn't want to think about it.

I eased along the rim until it gave way to layers of granite slabs snapped in two as tectonic plates shifted in millennia past, forming a stairway of sorts. I climbed down the granite to the base of the drop-off, where I discovered a slight overhang. The ground was covered with dry pine needles and pinecones.

It wasn't much, but it was more than I'd had two minutes earlier.

Quickly, before the light was gone, I scraped a small clearing at the base of the rocky overhang and laid the beginnings of a small fire using dry needles and pith I'd dug from some dead branches with my pocket knife.

Then I waited. From time to time, a voice drifted down, but soon darkness spread over the mountains and the voices faded away. I removed the fire starter from my zipper tab and opened it. Shivering against the cold, I waited until it was pitch black. In the darkness, I hit the striker several times against the steel rod of the fire starter. Brilliant sparks flew, and within moments, I had a tiny ember smoldering in my tiny pile.

I fed it more needles and a couple of pinecones, but they burned so quickly and so hot, I brushed them from the small fire, fearful Hymie or one of his goons might smell the smoke.

Later that night, huddled over my small fire and nibbling on some dried apples and apricots, I assessed my situation.

I didn't figure Hymie and his goons were out searching for me at night. I had no idea if or how badly the vehicles were damaged from bouncing down the rocky slope. Unfortunately for me, both vehicles appeared to have come to a halt on the road, which meant, if they were drivable, they were probably at the cabin at this very moment.

At first, I thought about going back to see, but I knew that would be impossible. I'd spent cloudy nights in forests and was well aware that without star- or moonlight, forests are darker than the inside of a cow.

No, I told myself, opening a package of organic mangoes. Wait until first light, and then head on down the mountain.

Huddling around the small fire, I slept in bits and pieces that night. I dozed in those witching hours of early morning, only to jerk awake at a foreign sound. I strained to listen. I peered up the slope just as the twin beams of headlights swung over my head and disappeared.

For a moment, I started to shout with joy but then I realized that the road above was the private one, and any vehicles there would belong to Hymie and his goons.

Moments later, car doors slammed and flashlights punched holes in the darkness on the mountain slope.

Fighting against panic, I started to break up my small fire, and then hesitated. Instead, I added several branches and pinecones to the fire. It blazed and, I hoped, would send enough smoke up the slope to draw Hymie down while I headed across the slope and attempted to come in behind the three. With luck, maybe I could steal a car. That was my only way out.

From high above, a voice shouted,"I smell smoke."

Hymie growled, "Shut up, dummy."

For the next several minutes, hands extended, I had to feel my way along. Behind and above, I spotted a single flashlight. I crouched behind a Volkswagen-sized boulder as the light passed almost a hundred yards north of me, heading for the source of the smoke.

By now, the first vestiges of light filtered through the pine and fir. Moving silently, I eased up the slope. Far above, I spotted the road. I grinned. Just another few minutes. I'd hotwired enough ignitions that I wasn't worried about starting either the Cadillac or the Ford. I could do either in mere seconds and be on my way.

I paused behind a pine just below the edge of the narrow road. A slow grin played over my lips. Hymie's Cadillac sat parked fifty yards up the road. I hesitated momentarily, remembering the Cadillac parked in the Zuider Zee parking lot. Hymie's was champagne colored, but the garish neon lights at the Zuider Zee prevented me from discerning the color except that the color was light.

Peering over my shoulder into the darkness of the forest below, I scrambled over the edge of the road and, dropping into a crouch, scurried to the far side, hoping to stay out of sight of those below. I hurried to the Cadillac, pausing before I touched it.

Hymie might not be a Rhodes Scholar, but the education he'd picked up in his line of work was just as comprehensive. There was no question in my mind that he had a PhD in CYTAAT, Covering Your Tail at All Times. So obviously he would have locked the Cadillac and set the alarm.

I grinned to myself when I peered through the window, studying the interior of the plush vehicle. I'd been right. The vehicle was locked tighter than my old man could hold on to a beer bottle.

If I'd had an ignition popper, I could smash the window, yank out the ignition, and wire it in less than fifteen seconds. But I didn't have the popper, so that meant I had to take the wiring from below the dash, another forty-five seconds at least.

Overhead a bird circled. I paid it no attention. Instead, I searched for a rock that would take care of the window. Suddenly, almost in my face, a brown and white bird about a foot long shot out from under one of the stones and zoomed past me.

With a startled shout, I jumped back. Seconds later, the frightened bird slammed into the Cadillac, and the emergency alarm began shrieking.

Shouts came from far below.

Muttering a heartfelt curse, I bolted down the road, heading for the forest beyond the switchback, hoping to find some type of alpine topography to camouflage my footprints.

Chapter Twenty-five

Once I reached the edge of the field of boulders and stepped into the forest, I paused and glanced back. None of the three had appeared yet on the road. Above me to my left rose a granite ledge forty feet high and extending a few hundred yards straight ahead to where it made a gradual curve back to the right, ending at the steep slope of an adjoining ridge.

Between me and the ridge lay a blanket of pristine snow covering a small valley almost three hundred yards wide. In the middle, there appeared to be a narrow depression running the length of the valley and disappearing into the forest below. I started across, and then hesitated, realizing my tracks would be obvious.

Picking my way around patches of snow, I angled back to the almost perpendicular walls of the ledge and, using fissures and chimneys in the face of the rock, scrambled to the top, where I quickly made my way to the far ridge, leaving no tracks on the windblown granite.

Pausing on the far ridge to gather my sense of direction, I guessed the main road was beyond and below the far side of the ridge on which I stood.

Suddenly, a distant voice jerked me around.

There, just emerging from the forest below, some three hundred yards distant, stood Maury Erickson, shaking a bony fist and, in his other hand, waving that .44 magnum at me.

I bolted for the crest of the ridge. At the same time, a distant pop echoed through the cold, frigid air, and off to my right, twenty yards or so, a small boulder exploded as a 240 grain slug impacted. I didn't even try to imagine what one of those slugs would do to me.

Hastily, I ducked behind a thick pine and peered around the side, the scaly bark scratching my face. Alex had appeared and seemed to be trying to hold Maury back. I couldn't help noticing they still wore their lightweight clothing. Stupid, I muttered to myself. Of course, why should they have worried? They figured they'd take care of me posthaste and then beat it out of here.

As I watched, the sepulcher figure jerked away from Alex and started across the snow-covered basin toward me.

Glancing over my shoulder, I searched for a larger tree. Although he was three hundred yards away, and handguns are notorious for inaccuracy at such a distance, there was always the possibility of chance, and lately, my chances had seemed to be running downhill.

On the slope about thirty feet above me was a thick-boled pine, thick enough to stop the seven or eight hundred foot-pounds of energy of the .44 slug. I glanced back at Maury.

He was bounding across the untouched snow in great leaps, and then one moment he was there, and the next, he'd vanished, deep into the snow.

All I heard was a drawn-out scream of terror.

Alex and Hymie rushed to him.

I didn't hang around. Five minutes later, I paused on the crest of the ridge and looked back down. Hymie, whose vehement cursing echoed through the jagged ridges of the

Sangre de Cristos, was peering down the hole while Alex struggled through the snow back to the Cadillac.

Without hesitation, I scrambled down the far side of the slope. At the base of the ridge, I came upon the crumbling cabin that marked the turnoff from the secondary road onto the private drive to the log house.

I thought about holing up inside, but quickly dismissed the idea. Not even those three were so stupid they wouldn't search it. I studied the cabin a few moments longer, thinking perhaps there might be something inside I could use.

I peered into the shadows of the long-deserted cabin. In every corner, I spotted pack rat nests. Half a dozen bunks lined the log walls, each long since ripped apart, but the one thing that remained were the ropes that supported the double-blanket mattresses the old-timers had used.

The ropes were tied in a checkerboard pattern, and I realized I could put them to use without a great deal of trouble or time, one of which I had too much of, and the other not enough.

Every Louisiana boy from the bayou prairies carries a pocketknife from the time he can walk. Mine was a three-blade Case given to me by my *grand-père* when I was eight. Of course, over thirty years of use had diminished the size of the blades. Mine weren't as thick as they had once been, but I kept them sharp enough to shave.

Quickly, I slashed the ropes free, threw them over my shoulder, and then vanished back into the forest, a crazy, insane idea in my head, which, if it succeeded, just might help me steal one of the cars. I shook my head and cautioned myself. *The smart thing to do, Tony, is to forget all this. Head down the road. You hear a car coming, hide!*

But I couldn't help remembering how Maury and the others were dressed, still in their lightweight clothes. They couldn't stay out in this weather too long without suffering frostbite. Me, I was dressed for it.

So, I convinced myself that if my zany idea worked, then I might live to prove that Carl Edwards was innocent and that he had been murdered by Frank Cooper and his thugs.

Well before the light faded from the forest, I'd found a cozy little niche deep in a fissure in the granite slabs comprising the great mountains.

Building a small torch, I explored several feet back into the opening, and to my surprise, stumbled onto a small chamber with the remnants of an ancient fire in one corner. For a moment, an eerie feeling swept over me as if somehow I had been caught up in a time warp primeval as the ages.

I built my fire in the same spot and later, from time to time as I cut and pieced the rope, I'd glance at the fire and wonder who might have sat exactly in my spot centuries earlier.

It was midnight by the time I finished. I sat back, nibbled on some dried apples, retrieved a couple of handfuls of snow from outside to wash it down, and leaned back, enjoying the warmth and security the fire offered.

While I wasn't exactly sure of my plans, I knew I was going to carry the fight to them. After all, Maury might be out of it. I had no idea what had happened to him. He had been there one moment, and the next he was gone. With any luck, I told myself, he'd dropped down into a ten-thousand-foot crevice.

I chuckled. My luck should be so good.

As soon as I could see enough to move through the forest the next morning, I shouldered my ropes and headed in the general direction of the log house at the top of the mountain.

*   *   *

An hour after the sun peered over the peaks back to the east, I crouched behind a thick tangle of understory vegetation, studying the house.

Smoke drifted up from one chimney.

Staying out of sight of the spacious log house, I circled around back, searching for an ideal spot to set my traps.

Millennia earlier, the forces of nature had shifted the massive tectonic plates beneath the surface, thrusting masses of granite into the air. The granite separated, leaving a thirty-foot-wide strip of soil a hundred yards in length between forty-foot upthrusts.

A well-used deer and elk trail wound through the pine and cedar filling the short pass. Around a bend in the trail, I set my first trap. Doubling the rope, I knotted it around a young pine, and then inserted a branch between the ropes so I could twist them, gaining leverage to bend the pine into an arc.

As a youth in the Louisiana swamps and prairies, I'd set more traps than I could count. All I had to do with this one was make it larger than a rabbit trap. I chuckled to myself. Someone was in for one heck of a surprise.

Dragging a ten-foot-long dead log to the far side of the trail, I tied a rope to either end, and then fastened them to the tip of the pine. I rigged a trip rope, a length of grapevine I'd cut from a nearby tangle, and covered it and the rope with pine needles.

I stepped back and studied the trap. In theory, it should work. Once the trip vine was hit, the pine would spring up, yanking the log across the trail and slamming it into whoever had been unlucky enough to trip the vine.

Drawing a deep breath, I glanced back toward the cabin. I'd planned another trap, but I'd used all my rope.

Moving on up the trail, I studied the almost perpendicular

granite walls on either side, searching for a spot to build a rockslide. Finding nothing, I turned my attention to locating two or three means of escape or hiding spots should my trap fail.

I found exactly what I was looking for where the trail made a sharp bend to the right. Back to the left was a fissure in the wall leading to the top of the ledge. Quickly I scrambled up, pausing at the top and looking around. "This'll do it," I muttered to myself, drawing in a breath of frigid air. If my trap worked as planned, I could hike back along the rim to the log house.

My stomach growled. I patted my pockets and discovered a small pack of carrot salad. I shook my head, muttering, "What I wouldn't give for a steak, or even a bowl of soup."

Opening the packet of carrot salad, I popped some in my mouth as I clambered back down the fissure. Now all I had to do was figure out how to get Hymie to follow me.

I didn't have to worry.

Alex took care of that for me.

Chapter Twenty-six

After reaching the base of the cliff, I headed back down the trail to the house. Rounding a bend, I jerked to a halt. Less than thirty feet in front of me stood a massive deer with antlers that would score sky-high in Boone and Crockett. He was sniffing at my trap.

I started to shout. That's all I needed, a lousy deer tripping the trap. But as soon as he spotted me, he bounced ten feet in the air and flip-flopped directions. When he landed, he was another thirty feet down the trail and streaking through the pines like a gunshot in the direction of the log house.

Breathing a sigh of relief, I skirted the trap and headed to the cabin, pausing just inside the forest at the edge of the clearing.

Quickly, I scanned the log house. The porch remained in shadows. I studied it when, suddenly, sunlight reflected off glass.

I don't know what prompted me, but I dropped instantly to my knees and rolled behind a pine as the booming roar of a deer rifle broke the silence, and a two-hundred-grain slug tore a chunk from the pine that I had been standing beside.

Alex shouted, "Hymie! It's Boudreaux. Out back. Quick!"

My pulse was racing from the close call. For a moment,

I remained frozen, trying to figure out how he'd spotted me so quickly. Then I realized he'd probably seen the spooked deer and grabbed his rifle, hoping for a shot.

Well, he got his shot, and no pun intended, but I dodged the bullet.

I turned and raced up the trail. Just before I sprinted around the first bend, I glanced back. Alex was halfway across the clearing, and Hymie was storming down the porch steps. Maury was nowhere in sight.

Slowing as I approached the next bend in the trail, I waited for Alex. I wanted to keep him on the trail, not go wandering off into the pines on either side.

When he spotted me, he threw the rifle to his shoulder, but I vanished. I grinned when I heard him cursing, "I'm going to nail your hide, Boudreaux!"

Ahead, I spotted the trap. I crossed my fingers as I leaped over the trip rope and raced to the next bend. Before I reached it, a deafening gunshot echoed down the trail. A small pine at my shoulder exploded and fell across the trail behind me.

Alex whooped. "Next time, Boudreaux. Next—Yahhhh—" A startled scream cut off his words as the whooshing of the pine whipped through the surrounding trees.

I didn't break stride until I cut off the trail and scrambled up the fissure to the top of the ledge.

From down below came screams of pain mixed with impassioned cursing. I plopped down on my belly and peered over the rim.

Alex lay on the edge of the trail, the heavy log resting on his chest. He was screaming, "Hymie! Get it off. Get it off."

But every time Hymie touched the log, Alex would scream again. "Easy, easy. My ribs are busted. Take it easy."

"Shut up," Hymie growled. "Once I get it off, it'll stop hurting." With that, he gripped one end of the log. "When I lift it, scoot out."

Alex bobbed his head once. "Hurry."

"Here goes." Hymie started to lift the log, but his fingers slipped on the wet bark, and the log fell back on Alex, who shrieked in pain, and then broke into a stream of curses.

Scooting away from the rim, I headed back to the cabin. For all I knew, Maury was dead, still buried in the snow, but I had to somehow get one of the cars. Behind me, I heard the screams and profanities spewing from the two goons.

I approached the massive log house from the rear, slipping onto a closed-in porch that opened into a spacious but rustic kitchen. The house was cold, and I realized the generator wasn't running.

I tiptoed to the door on the opposite wall and peered into a large room, the same one in which I first came face to face with Hymie. An almost overpowering silence, more fitting to a mausoleum than a vacation house, filled the room.

Straining for the slightest sound, I heard nothing.

Suddenly, the ceiling above my head squeaked. I froze. Someone was on the second floor. I looked around for some kind of weapon. Beside the fire pit sat a wrought-iron tool set. I grabbed the poker and headed for the stairs, which were, as I remembered the layout of the house, in the next room.

I paused to glance out the window. Still no sign of Hymie and Alex.

Opening the heavy slab doors a crack, I peered into the next room. It was empty, so I quickly hurried to the stairs and slipped up to the second floor. The upstairs hallway looked down on the spacious room below.

Easing along the thick puncheon floor, I paused at each closed door and listened. At the third door, I heard a groan, and then the bed squeaked.

I caught my breath and closed my eyes in an effort to still my racing pulse. I flexed my fingers about the poker, and then slowly turned the knob. The door opened soundlessly. I peered inside and spotted Maury Erickson lying under several tousled blankets, his eyes closed, a sheen of sweat glistening on his face, and a soft moan on his lips. A half-full bottle of bourbon sat on the nightstand.

I eased inside, the poker drawn back over my head.

The floor creaked.

His eyes opened. A thick glaze covered them. He stared at me, seeing nothing. "Hymie? Is that you? You got to help me, Hymie. My leg's busted. I can feel the bone sticking out. I got fever from infection. I gotta have a doctor."

I lowered my voice to match the tenor of Hymie's. "Yeah. Okay. Just sleep."

Quickly, I searched the room for Maury's .44 magnum, but found nothing. I had turned to leave when I heard the front door slam shut.

Hymie!

Moving quickly, I opened the door a crack and peered down below. My heart skipped a beat when I spotted Hymie climbing the stairs. I looked around, frantically searching for someplace to hide. I glanced at the closet. Before I could move, his footsteps stopped just outside the door.

I gulped when the doorknob turned. With the poker above my head, I backed up against the wall behind the door as it swung open.

Hymie growled. "We're back, Maury."

A moment of lucidity swept over Maury. "Hymie? But—But you was just here."

That was my signal to get out of there.

I leaped past Hymie into the hall, slammed the door behind me, and pressed up against the wall by the door. The fat was in the fire, as they say, and the next couple of minutes would see if I lived or died.

Chapter Twenty-seven

Hymie pounded across the floor, jerked open the door, and barged into the hall waving his automatic.

I slammed the poker down on his hand, knocking the piece to the floor and sending it skittering over the edge of the hall to the room below. Unfortunately, the impact jarred the poker from my hand, and it followed the automatic to the floor below.

Hymie cursed and grabbed his hand. He glared at me. "I'm gonna bust you in two." Though the cold-eyed killer was a couple of inches shorter than me, he had me by fifty pounds, and I couldn't see an ounce of fat on him. He doubled his fists and charged me, swinging both arms wildly.

I ducked under his charge and, making both hands into a single fist, slammed him in the back, driving him into the log wall.

He bounced off and hit the floor, blood pouring from his flattened nose. His eyes blazed as he struggled to his feet.

Fighting is not my forte. And to me, "fair fighting" has to be the world's number one oxymoron. As he tried to stand, I hit him in the forehead with my fist. I grimaced, figuring I had broken something, and not his hard head.

He fell back on the floor, rolled onto his stomach, and pushed to his feet. Blood continued streaming from his nose, staining his rumpled jacket. He bared his teeth and snarled,

"You're a dead man, Boudreaux." And he launched his muscular body at me.

No way on earth could I have stood toe-to-toe with Hymie Weinshank. He was a bull, and an enraged one at that. Your own blood covering the floor will do that to you.

He threw a right that rocked me back on my heels. A gleam of triumph filled his eyes, and he hit me with a wild left that spun me back into the rugged log walls. My head banged off the wall and stars exploded behind my eyes.

For a moment, the blows raining on me stopped. I shook my head, trying to clear it. Hymie had turned from me and was searching the hallway floor for his automatic. I stepped forward and, grabbing his arm, spun him around, at the same time throwing as hard a straight right as I could.

I caught him on the tip of his chin. His head jerked back, and I swung a left, aiming for his exposed throat, but I missed. My momentum spun me around, and when I looked back, Hymie had lowered his bull-like head and lunged at me. I tried to step aside, but I slipped in his blood and fell. His impetus carried him over me. He tripped on my leg.

And he disappeared over the top of the stairs.

I jumped to my feet and ran to the stairs, ready to throw myself at him if he were trying for his automatic. I jerked to a halt and gaped at the motionless body lying at the base of the stairs.

Jeez, I told myself instinctively, *I hope I didn't kill the guy.*

He was still alive. Taking no chances, I tied him securely.

I found Alex on the porch, spitting up blood from his busted ribs that had obviously punctured his lungs. Despite his pain, I complimented myself with a grin for fashioning such an effective trap with next to nothing to work with.

After securing their weapons, I helped Alex inside, and then dragged the still unconscious Hymie down the front steps by his feet, taking a perverted delight in letting the back of his head bang off each step. Then I managed to heft him into the trunk of the Ford Taurus.

I looked down at Alex. "I'm going for a doctor. If you leave here, you'll die. You need a hospital. Same for Maury upstairs. You understand?"

Clenching his teeth, he looked up at me through pain-filled eyes. "Yeah, yeah. Just hurry back."

The sheriff at Lost Lake stuck Hymie in a cell and sent the local paramedics out to the Carmony place. "I'm leaving this feller in here just until I get this straightened out," he announced, his light blue eyes giving me a piercing glare. "I got no idea what's going on, but I'll blasted well get to the bottom of it. I ain't one of your city boys that has to go around making sure none of the local politicians ain't going to have their little love lives all messed up." He nodded to a chair beside his desk. "Now suppose you start."

When I finished, he leaned back and studied me. The lines in his craggy face ran together in concentration. "It sounds mighty pretty, mighty well pieced together, but you got no hard proof. All them fellers got to do is deny they told you anything."

I grinned. "Don't worry, sheriff. I got me an ace in the hole."

Five minutes later, I played it.

The sheriff and I looked at Hymie through the cold, iron bars of the cell. The sheriff explained my accusations. Hymie grinned—no, he sneered, and then said, "Sheriff, I don't know what he's talking about. Me and my friends was taking a little vacation. One started to fall off a cliff and the other one grabbed him. That's how they both got hurt." He gave me a sly grin.

I stepped forward. "What about Copper Canyon, Hymie? You remember Copper Canyon, don't you?"

He stared at me in defiance. "I never heard of it." I had to hand it to him. He was carrying his bluff right down to the last period in the sentence.

A faint grin ticked up one side of my lips. "No? What do you want to bet Maury and Alex have heard about it?"

He dragged the tip of his tongue over his dry lips and shot a nervous glance at the sheriff. "I don't know what you're talking about."

I shrugged. "No? Well, we'll ask Maury and Alex. I got a feeling they're hurting so bad right now that the last thing they want to do is take the fall for you and Cooper, especially if he's going to make off with the half million."

The sheriff looked at me in surprise, and then glared accusingly at Hymie, who grabbed the bars and, clenching his teeth, glared at me. If looks could have killed, I would have been burned to a crispy critter right then. After several moments, however, his shoulders slumped. He staggered back a couple of steps and plopped down on the hard bunk and buried his face in his hands. "What do you want to know?"

Chapter Twenty-eight

Chief Pachuca frowned up at me when I entered his office. His eyes slid over the new knot on my forehead. He shook his head. "So, what kind of trouble did you cause me now?"

After he heard my story, he called D.A. Investigator Mark Swain over and made me repeat it.

When I finished, Pachuca handed Mark a thick packet. "Here are their confessions incriminating Frank Cooper of the Tri-County Credit Union, signed and sealed by the appropriate law officials of Cristo County, New Mexico. Sheriff Garcia sent them by Boudreaux here."

Swain pursed his lips. "You mentioned a Rita Johnson at the credit union." He held up the packet. "Is she in here?"

"No." I hesitated, trying to pick my words. "I don't know how she is involved with Cooper. I do know she's the one who steered me to Lost Lake. She said Edwards had fished up there often, but no one knew him. I'll wager Cooper put her up to it. And," I added, "the armored car guards said someone came in and left before Edwards came in. It could have been her."

Swain glanced at Pachuca. "Can you pick Cooper up for me, Chief?"

182

"No problem," he replied, reaching for the phone. "At the same time, I'll send a unit out to Copper Canyon."

Swain studied me a moment, and then waved the packet at me and with a grin, said, "I'll take care of it. If I need you, I'll call. Looks like this clears your father."

"Yeah," I replied. "Until next time."

He laughed.

After Swain left, Pachuca looked up at me with an expression that looked half impatient and half amused. "Well, Boudreaux. As I see it, you didn't break any of my rules, but you sure bent a couple of them like pretzels."

I was not sure just how he meant it, but I decided to take his remark as a compliment. "Thanks, Chief."

He nodded curtly. "Just don't do it again, you hear?"

The Edwards were my next stop. I dreaded it even though I told myself Debbie and her mother expected the worst.

They took the news with a sense of relief. "At least now we know," Mrs. Edwards muttered, dabbing at the tears rolling down her cheeks. "We expected as much, but now—"

Debbie wrapped her arm around her mother's shoulders. "Now we know, Mom. Now we can get on with our lives." She looked up at me. "I just can't believe Frank Cooper was behind it. And to think he shot himself to put the blame on Dad." Tears welled in her eyes.

I grinned crookedly. "He almost got away with it."

She smiled at me gratefully. "He would have if it hadn't been for you, Tony."

"Well," I replied, glancing at my watch. "If I'm not mistaken, Frank Cooper is on the way down to the police station as we speak."

A faint smile ticked up her lips. She laid her hand on mine. "Thank you, for everything."

I squeezed her hand. "You're a wonderful woman, Debbie. Just remember, anytime you or your mother need anything, let me know."

She studied me for several moments, a sad smile on her lips and regret in her eyes. I guess she knew then our time had passed. Finally she nodded. "Thank you—" She paused, and then added, "Friend."

I felt like a heel.

After leaving the Edwards, I picked up my old man and his backpack, which I guessed Danny had bought him. I gave him a hundred bucks and, at his request, dropped him off on Sixth Street in front of the Limestone Pawn Shop. "You're welcome to stay. You know that, John Roney," I said before he closed the pickup door.

He slung the backpack over his shoulder. "I got itchy feet, boy. Besides, I'm supposed to meet a man up in Fort Worth. Business deal."

The rail yard was several blocks from Sixth Street. "I can drive you over there."

"Nah. There's a couple old boys here I want to tell good-bye." Without another word, he closed the door and stepped back.

With a mixture of relief and disappointment, I stared at him another few seconds, and then pulled away from the curb into the traffic. I glanced in the rearview mirror. He was still standing at the curb.

That night, I was sitting on the couch, nibbling on a sausage pizza and sipping a glass of nonalcoholic cherry cider when the phone rang. It was Danny. "Hey, Tony, is your old man still around?"

Naïve me, I should have figured something was wrong, but I didn't. "Nope. He hopped a freight to Fort Worth. Why? What's up?"

"I'm missing a brass statue of Diana."

I frowned. "Diana? Diana who?"

He sputtered, "Dummy! Diana—the Roman goddess of the hunt. I had one in my office, and now she's gone."

For a couple of moments, I sat like a wooden dummy with a brain to match, and then I realized what had happened. "Would it fit in a backpack?"

"Yeah. Why?"

I shook my head. That's why that conniving old man of mine wanted me to drop him off at the pawnshop. That's why he didn't want me to drive him to the rail yard. I closed my eyes and drew a deep breath.

Danny spoke up. "Tony! You still there? Hey!"

"Yeah. I'm here. How much was that thing worth, Danny?"

"Huh?"

"I think I know where it is. How much would a pawn-broker give for it?"

He hesitated, and then chuckled. "Fifty bucks, maybe."

"Tell you what. I'll drop it off in the morning, okay?"

"Okay." He laughed.

"Sorry."

"Don't sweat it."

I called Chesed Kaber at Limestone Pawn Shop. I had no idea what the name Kaber meant, but old Chesed had told me more than once his given name meant *mercy*, which from his dealing with his clients was the last thing

I ever saw him display. I arranged to pick it up the next morning.

That night, I slept the sleep of the innocent. The only problem I now faced was begging Janice's forgiveness for missing the car show.